My Own Sweet Time

My Own Sweet Time

Wanda Koolmatrie

Magabala Books

First published by Magabala Books Aboriginal Corporation
Broome Western Australia 1994

Magabala Books receives financial assistance from the State Government
of Western Australia through the Department for the Arts; the Aboriginal
and Torres Strait Islander Commission; and the Aboriginal and Torres Strait
Islander Arts Board of the Australia Council, the Federal Government's arts
funding and advisory body. Grateful acknowledgement is made for the
support of Apple Computer Australia.

Designer Narelle Jones
Editors Rachel Bin Salleh, Peter Bibby
Production Grant Drage
Printed by Frank Daniels, Perth
Typeset in Sabon 11/14pt

National Library of Australia
Cataloguing-in-Publication data

Koolmatrie, Wanda, 1949-.

    My Own Sweet Time

    ISBN 1.875641 22 X.

    I. Title.

    A 823.3

Cover art: Sam Cook

Department for
theArts
Government of Western Australia

Australia Council
for the Arts

Contents

I look as if I'm winning because I
am alive but I am in the same
night as you

Albert Camus, Notebooks

Part 1

By six years old I'd picked up a handful of stunts — bawling out for milk and porridge, recognizing animals and visitors, responding to my parents with coyness, indifference, enthusiasm, whatever. Cause and effect were tumbling into a pattern. One thing puzzled me though. Mum and Dad and the few people who came to the house were all white. I knew no other children. I was certainly growing, but I stayed black. Would I fade, or what?

School had been mentioned off and on for maybe a year or so. It would be like this: every day I would get up early, just like Dad, and leave the house, a thing I'd never done, and Mum would take me to a castle full of kids, and someone would stand up in front of us and tell us how to live and what to do, and what had happened in the world so far, and how to read stories by ourselves, and draw even better than I could already, and count past fifty, and catch a ball. Also how to sing, if I was good. It sounded like a bargain to me. All this was now payable, the day had come.

Dad had shambled off to work with his kitbag full of tools and sandwiches, the dog had settled down again and Mum was stuffing apples and things into my new case. I had sharp crayons and hardly any patience. The chain came off the wooden gate. This on its own would have justified the circle on the calendar. Up till now the world beyond our hedge had been no more real than stuff in picture books. Not that I doubted its existence. I knew there were lions and tigers out there, and Jesus, followed by crowds of kids, some of them like me and some white like grown ups. This last detail had alarmed me at first, but I'd only been about four then, and hadn't realised you could do anything you like with coloured pencils.

Now came the bombshell. I'd known there'd be a million brats in the street, kids in the same boat as me. But fancy dress hadn't been mentioned. Some had orange hair and spots like Dad, and there was yellow hair, and even the black haired ones had white faces. They all had white skin. All sorts of bizarre combinations, but they all had white skin.

"You didn't tell me *this*, Mum!"

"What, dear?"

I was in no mood to be raw prawned.

"Why didn't you doll me up like them?"

"Don't be silly. Come on."

You could hear the playground racket from our joint. It had hypnotised me for years. Now it got louder. Mum dragged me along by the wrist. Gigglers and bullies seemed to agree that I was centre stage.

2

There was pointing and shouting — something about 'Golly'. I felt like spewing by the time we made it to the Castle. I'd been stooged alright. And here was the teacher. Huge and wrinkled. She stuck me in the front row.

I'd woken up to things by now of course. There was no grease paint, no powder. This crowd was white and I was the only black kid in the world. Imagine Mum and Dad keeping it under their hats so long, like it was a detail or something. I couldn't believe it. Tonight I'd run question time, but right now it was teacher's turn. 'Miss Gibbon' she chalked up with a shaky line under it. "I'm Miss Gibbon," she admitted. A few kids laughed. I knew about gibbons too but kept a straight face. I had weirder stuff to chew on. We'd all been given bits of cardboard with pins through them. Miss Gibbon circled the room printing names on the cards and sticking them to our clothes. There were lots of Johns and Julies and Kevins but I was the only Wanda. Plus I'd written it myself, like Mum had shown me. Everyone laughed except Miss Gibbon. She seemed pleased.

We were allowed to draw for a while, then a rough-looking big kid delivered a crate of milk which we all had to help scoff, unless we had a note from home. Then there was more drawing until lunch time. This hour was the hardest bit. Gangs formed at once. I guess some of the kids already knew each other, but maybe not. Chasing games started up but they didn't look much to me. I found a bench under a tree and started wolfing down my fish paste. The milk boy came up with a pod full of itchy stuff and tipped it down my back.

The afternoon was crammed with numbers and building blocks. By the time Mum came to get me the others weren't staring quite so much. I guess nothing's funny over and over again. Jerry Lewis maybe.

Nothing much was said on the way home. Mum seemed a bit tense, but I wasn't feeling helpful. I'd wait till Dad got back, and corner them together. The dog kicked up as usual when the gate squeaked. Mum went inside to shell the peas. I mucked around behind the shed disturbing spiders and stuff. All sorts of theories occurred to me. What if I stayed black forever? It seemed possible, even likely. Maybe I wouldn't ever grow up. What then? Could I stay here with Mum? And what about school? Clearly I'd be taken there every day. What for? Boys went to school until they turned into blokes, like Dad. Girls turned into their mums in the end, but would I do that? And if not? My education had begun but there were even more questions than I'd had the day before. Hard ones too.

Dad was making cubes and pyramids out of his mashed potato. Before now he'd always bolted his food and rushed off to the wireless. He knew it wasn't an ordinary day, but he wouldn't break the silence, I could tell. Same with Mum — apart from saying grace, nothing. They didn't even ask about school. I knew guilt when I saw it close up.

"No one else is black, Mum."

Dad jumped up straight away. For months he'd been meaning to oil that gate.

"Mum?" I'd never seen her this pale.

"Go into your room dear, I'll be with you directly." She meant after the dishes.

"Tell me Mum." She started clearing the table. Pretty slowly it seemed. Anyway, it got done. She took off her apron and sat down with me. I didn't push any more, I knew she was trapped.

"You're a big girl now, Wanda. I probably should have said something. You know Daddy and I care for you and so does Jesus…"

She was rambling. She was all over the shop. I stared at a scratch on the table. Mum kept talking until she said something.

"…and if it weren't for us, you'd be living in the sand eating worms and catching a cold, but Pastor Preston found you and brought you to Jesus and gave you clothes and food and a mummy and daddy."

It was a day's work, but eventually I had some kind of outline. Part of it was good news. There were in fact other black people. They were called Aborigines. But apparently they were like naughty kids even though they'd grown up. They threw sticks at each other and didn't have a clue about Jesus or anything. Aborigines messed around for their whole life and couldn't write their name. But fortune had snatched me from this morbid scene, and delivered me to the suburbs of Adelaide. My real father was a white bloke, a shearer. He couldn't be found. And so on. Mum's diagram of my history.

She took me off to bed after unloading this data. She brought cocoa and raved for ages about this and that. Jesus mainly, but also a lot of domestic stuff, like I was suddenly grown up. She crept out when I shut my eyes. I pottered among the revelations for a while, then I guess I dozed off.

Home was a breeze for a long time after this. Not that I'd ever had a rough time there, but now everything was more relaxed. I'd seen my universe twisted, but I made a point of sticking to my habits. Dad especially laughed more and even started taking me for sidecar rides. For a while he kept mumbling something about water and a duck's back, and Mum shook her head and couldn't stop grinning. It was an easy trot for sure.

Strangers of course still gazed at me but I just figured they knew my story, how I'd been dragged from the wreck and given a chance. Aborigines weren't mentioned again. I wondered where they hung out and what would happen if I ran into them. Maybe they'd snatch me back from Mum and carry me away. Where to? Did they have cars or what? Nothing made sense and I knew I couldn't ask. Not even Miss Gibbon.

She was pretty friendly because I did all my work and didn't give her a hard time. But she wouldn't know about black people, I could tell. She always tilted her head at me and pulled a dreamy face. She meant well, I think, but it was kind of like a doctor and patient scene. You couldn't forget who had the upper hand. I've run into this approach again and again over the years. It seems to be the only alternative to straight out heckling, apart from a complete snubbing of course, which is the least offensive.

Luckily, most of the kids at school opted for the snub, after their initial shock. One boy stands out among the exceptions, a certain Trevor. He was a complete horror show, even worse than the milk boy. This Trevor was red headed and fierce looking, at least eight years old I'd say. It was his third shot at Miss Gibbon's course and he was still getting it wrong. I couldn't believe it. Not that I was top of the class, but I was close, and this, plus my colour, drove Trevor nuts. He chucked spitballs at me, put dead flies in my lunch box, pulled my hair, called me Tar-face. Classic warfare in short. He wasn't much, but even the least competent mosquito gets to you after a while, and you lash out.

His pale blue stare had been on me for months, but I knew his rituals too, he wouldn't get away. After school he was invariably first out of the room, first up the alley, and always running. At afternoon recess one day I sneaked out and set up a wire, ankle height. It worked. Picture it, you don't need Sam Pekinpah. Quietly out for Trevor. I think he transferred to an Opportunity School after his recovery. Oddly enough, I spotted him years later, playing in a rock band. It was him for sure, right there under the strobe. Maybe I'd done him a favour, who knows?

I'd had my first taste of solo flight. I don't think I'm a vicious type, but it was milk and honey, I may as well say. Even Miss Gibbon couldn't have squared things so well. Other stuff would have been dragged in. Somehow I would have found myself on the carpet. This is how it always went as soon as a third party interfered, whether by invitation or not. One against one was cleaner, less complicated. I felt almost respected after Trevor had gone. Maybe it was just my new confidence. On the other hand, the kids had probably been able to put two and two together. I would hope so — we'd been at school for several months.

* * *

There were subtle changes at home over the next few years. My questioning had of course got sharper, but I still got the same responses from Mum — Yes dear, no dear, that's nice dear, as if I were still an infant, easy to shake or subdue. Sometimes her answers didn't make sense. I'd set her up with grotesque riddles off the top of my head. Somewhere I'd heard the chilling expression 'Boong'.

"Mum, why did the chicken cross the boong?"

"Yes dear."

She was out the window alright. It was fun at first, flinging absurdities around. I even made up new words.

"Askadandra, and ask me another."

"If you like, dear."

She was never on the ball like she'd been in the old days. Jesus and charity took up her life. She seemed to have lost interest in everything else. Even me. Mum's religion had become completely personal, and her welfare work consisted of sorting junk for unknown recipients. She was kind of like a hermit. Even Dad was somewhere outside her thoughts. He had his wireless and didn't seem to mind. He liked Jesus okay, I guess, and so did I for that matter, but I finally figured there was plenty of other stuff to look at.

This sprawling monotone had one gleaming aspect though. I was free to conjure up my own angles, learn what I liked and chuck the nonsense overboard. School work seemed like a waste of time in itself, but it was pretty easy, so I ripped through it anyway to keep everyone quiet. I didn't feel like repeating any years, like some of those hoods had to do. They strutted around and talked too loud, but I could tell they were mugs. Who'd want to be the class veteran? I nearly always got my homework done straight away, and bolted from the house while it was still light. Mum was usually out, or else caught up in her daydream or whatever it was. Dad often worked late, but even at home he stayed in the shed tampering with bits of wire and glass tubes. He'd collected a whole lot of books about radio and TV repairs. He thought he might start up his own racket. He wasn't sure yet.

Sometimes he just sat there drinking tea and gazing at his motorbike. I don't know what he thought about. It was a bit like Mum and Jesus in a way, but at least he'd answer questions. If it got dark too early, or rained or something, and I didn't feel like my daily prowl, grilling Dad was an option. He'd have a shot at any subject, and never waved me away.

I guess he was part bluff, but that didn't matter. Talk was talk, and from him I picked up details I may not have spotted on my own. Once I nailed him on the topic of foreign languages. There were lots of immigrants at school, and the stuff I heard when their mums picked them up knocked me out with its mystery and speed. Dad said just about every country had its own lingo. I'd seen plenty of maps. The claim seemed outrageous.

"Could I learn to talk like the paperboy?"

"Italian? Why not? It takes years though!"

"What if I wanted to know every language?"

"Ha! Impossible. I was in Paris after the war, but I don't know more than ten words of French."

"Say them."

"They're not for you, curly top."

A dead end. Dad still saw me as a punk. I wondered whether My People had their own patter. I'd started referring mentally to Aborigines as My People. It seemed romantic. It made me feel almost grown. Well, I was. Eleven years old is a key chapter of *anyone's* odyssey. But it wasn't a good moment to bite Dad for answers.

Anyway, he'd stirred my curiosity, better than nothing. I shambled out to the street. It still looked sepia, even at this traditionally vivid hour. Dust loitered everywhere. The sun may have dropped already, you couldn't tell. The cloud was dense, but there was no action. No rain, or even a breeze. No one else was around. It felt almost like a ghost town, with nothing moving except a curtain here and there. What sordid rubbernecks they were, still peering at me after all this time, like I'd been some nameless cut-throat dragging a parachute.

It was all in my head, I knew that, just a rough day for some reason. All the same, I felt like getting out of my district. Miles out. I could walk into the city for instance. This had been outlawed by Mum and Dad, but not recently. What did it matter, anyway? I'd outgrown their quaint set-up. Not that I saw them as enemies or anything, but what can you learn from watching people on the border of sleep? Obscure medical details maybe. That wasn't my line.

I got to the open end of our cul-de-sac. A French expression, someone had commented. Was it in Dad's vocab? Was it one word or three? This kind of tomfoolery must have tangled my thoughts for quite a while. I found myself right up near the railway depot before I'd even noticed anything else. I hadn't been this far on foot before.

Leaning on the grimy fence of the bridge, I watched the blokes mucking around in the shunting yard. The engines picked their teams and off they went. Diesels had started to replace steam. Exotic symbols plastered the carriages and no one had a clue where they went. At least, no one that I knew. A whistle and a certain flag, and off they lurched. Off to the desert maybe, or another town.

Even Sydney. I'd seen a picture of Sydney. A teacher had shown it to me one day, I forget the context. Early settlers probably. It had sailing ships and guys prodding at chained-up crooks, but what struck me most was a group of black people on a hill in the foreground. I didn't have to ask twice.

"Aborigines, Wanda."

A glimpse at last. They did have sticks, as I'd heard, and their garments weren't sharp. But no one had thought to mention their majesty. They stood like they owned the joint. Tough, athletic, proud. But pensive too, and perhaps a bit sad. In brief, heroes.

This recollection helped me to shake my flat mood. I dug a bush biscuit out of my shirt and kept watching the trains. They were hooking up a string of boxcars and a few cages for sheep and cattle. A couple of oil tanks too. I'd heard of people hopping slow freights like this one, and waking up free. I hadn't thought much about my career. This hobo thing blazed out like a full page ad. I'd keep it on the burner anyway. I'd learn a bit more, then I'd slink out of town by night.

Corny? So what. I was only eleven. It can't have been long after this, that I started up a kind of journal. The early pages have been lost, but I think it was that same year. I *do* remember how the idea kicked off. I used to make things up at the drop of a hat. Sometimes I'd mutter them out loud. A mistake. Strangers can get away with it. People just button their coats and hurry on. But talking to yourself upsets those you know. It's taken as an insult or something.

This happened once or twice with girls at school, and my scribbling habit emerged. It started out with kidstuff of course. Rags-to-riches, with me in the driver's seat. That may have lasted a few weeks, I can't remember, but soon

I got the rhyming bug. I started reducing my passing notions to verse. Sing song rubbish no doubt, but it kept me lively. I've dabbled in poems ever since. My impression of the world as a sepia print persisted. Quiet horror continued to coat my life. I soon realized I'd have to bolt from Adelaide. But I also knew that a runaway kid wouldn't last a day. Especially me, the walking side-show. No use thinking about it. Until the age of sixteen or so, I faked an interest in the beaten track. And I kept my trap shut.

***

For my parents' generation, sacrifice in wartime was a standard thing. Freedom and honour were to be protected. Louts who thought they could jackboot over us had collected bodgie data. We'd fight, and if we died, we died. But Vietnam was a bit curlier. Someone else's turf, a foreign squabble. Should our strapping youth stick its neck out? "Probably not," was the growing response. Eventually the discontent became a chant. "Peace now" et cetera. At first it was a bunch of art students playing Ghandi at Parliament House. "We'll eat when the troops come home." Something like that. Peak hour was amused, the police swept up, the status quo cleared its throat and put its feet up again. That's all folks. But it wasn't.

Support appeared from unlikely corners. Academics began to back up their apprentices. Thirty year-olds shuffled up to the mike. Some punters recognised an epic in the making. There was plenty of limelight. If you couldn't sing, you danced. Meanwhile the hippie business was filtering in. Smirks and petals everywhere. And dope of course. Plenty was upturned and everything else wobbled.

Some people were blasé, they'd seen it in the planets. Others gazed bewildered at the TV news.

Things were lively enough to hold me for a few months after school had finished. I didn't go home much. At that time you could flop anywhere. Even strangers didn't flinch. There was a kind of ramshackle unity. The new etiquette was pretty strict in its way, and there was overkill for sure, but who cared? It was a milestone.

The Beatles, I guess, had already kicked over a couple of walls to open the show. But this New Age thing outstripped any teenage cult, however raucous. That's how people saw it, a New Age. Out with the bath water. Not a bad idea. I've been trying to count up the houses I stayed in that year. About a dozen I think, any two of them interchangeable. A grubby mattress, a loud poster with writhing hieroglyphs legible only to the drug crazed. Curtains were unheard of. It all passed for minimalism, but was probably sloth.

In mid-December of '67 I decided I'd spend Christmas with Mum and Dad and then hop on a train for Melbourne. With a ticket, that is. Like I said, I hadn't been home very often since I left school, and those odd times had been at night. I guess I was vaguely curious the morning I turned into our street. There'd been no revolution here. I don't know what I expected after only a few months, but anyway, here it was. The same chatter at the same gates. And mongrels coughing out the same tired riffs. Here it was, the ancient refrain, dot for dot.

Dad was kneeling under the fig tree with a toothbrush and a carburettor. He was working on his now fashionable wartime Harley. Apparently, even the normally contemptuous Douglas twins from over the road stopped to admire it now and then.

13

"G'day."

"Hi Wanda. What's new?"

"Not much. I thought I might go to Melbourne. Live there I mean."

"Melbourne? What for?"

"Changes, opportunities. You know."

"What's wrong with Adelaide?"

"It's okay. I want to look around, that's all."

"Well, your room's here whenever you want it, but you know that."

"Thanks Dad, but I feel like a kid when I come back. Everything's exactly the same, the whole street."

"Not the Workshop." This is what we called the old quilt factory on the corner.

"Is it running again?"

"No, no. Someone's living there, communists I think. They don't even pay rent. They just arrived in a truck about a month ago. There's some kind of loophole, and no one can touch 'em."

"Are they noisy, or what?"

"Not really. Weird music sometimes, but it's not that. It couldn't have happened ten years ago."

"They're probably hippies."

"Ha! Still the romantic. This isn't America."

"No, I s'pose not... Where's Mum?"

"In the shed painting toys. Beyond repair most of 'em, but you know Mum."

"I'll go and see. Can I stay here for a couple of weeks?"

"Of course, I told you. Don't mention Melbourne. We'll smuggle it in at tea time."

Mum was scraping the rust off a once flashy tip truck. She was humming *Twist and Shout*. Maybe she thought it was about martyrdom. "I'm home, Mum."

"Hello dear. Now you're still young. Should I use red or blue on this?"

"You know best Mum. How have you been?"

"Ah, much the same. Have you seen Dad?"

"Yeah, I spoke to him in the yard. How much have you got to do?"

"God's work doesn't end, Wanda."

"Dad said you've got new neighbours."

"Hm? Ah yes, the Munchkins. The poor dears, I take them soup. Don't tell your father. Those children eat like horses when they can. It's not enough though, they always look tired. Yet they can't be much older than you. One of them smokes a pipe, like an old man."

I didn't know where to look. I settled for the pile of busted dolls.

"Do you need any help with this stuff?"

"No thank you dear, I'm on schedule I think. Are you staying tonight?"

"Yeah, if that's okay. You sure I can't do something?"

"You could run down to Boltons' for some corned beef."

"Okay, see you in a minute."

The street was quiet. People had gone inside. There was the Workshop with its broken windows. It looked the same, despite its teeming populace.

I won't bother to outline Christmas at home. But New Year's Eve had its moments. Dad drank two bottles of beer and told us about Paris in the '40s. Mum played the organ for a while. Her brother Vince turned up unannounced. I didn't remember him at all. He lived in Queensland and played in a Latin-type band. He was down here for a season at the Lido. Or the Trocadero. Somewhere like that. He was due on stage at eleven and had called in to visit us on his way. He was already dressed. Velvet suit and dyed hair. Clip-on bow tie sticking from his top pocket. 'The Wondrous Vincenzo' he called himself. He dug out his emerald coloured guitar and scooted up and down the neck. Like ringing a bell, Dad said.

Uncle Vince was slick enough, there's no dodging that. He played *Quiet Nights,* and bits he'd made up. Dad was impressed. Mum smiled politely. It wasn't my kind of music, but I knew mastery when I saw it. Just the same, I had my own two bob's worth ready.

"Can I have a shot, Uncle?" Nearly everyone I knew had picked up a couple of guitar chords. I'd learnt five.

"Okay, but don't drop it or I'll have to get a job, ha, ha."

I'd recently put one of my poems to music. Well, three chords anyway. I strummed a sort of intro and half talked the lyrics. I'm no songbird, but everyone cheered anyway. Even Mum. It felt like a flying dream, I won't play it down. I didn't have an encore ready but I'd got the bug alright. Songwriting I mean, not performance. That wouldn't have suited me at all. Not in public.

Uncle Vince left in a cab. Dad rambled some more about Europe and the great dance bands from the old days. We had cocoa and sponge cake. At midnight we went out in the yard to hear people blow their horns. Dad revved up his bike. Then we all went inside. Even the dog. It was over a hundred now in human years. The racket gradually died down, except for a timeless raga blaring from Munchkins Villa.

* * *

16

A week or so later I was arranging my pillow on the Overland, the express to Melbourne. I'd asked my parents not to see me off. Mum had grumbled a bit. Other people I hadn't even told. Acquaintances from the various flops. No one cared for plans. You were supposed to 'go with the flow', or make it look that way. A prepaid rail ticket would have been uncool. Worse than a pocket full of cash, in a way. I had that too. About sixty dollars. A couple of bob a week in the school bank turns into something after a while.

Just before the train was due to start I heard shouting on the platform. A bearded guy was being hauled off by the cops. "Pigs," he kept saying, and "Fascist murderers." Stuff like that. I knew the script. He was supposed to be in the army but had other ideas. Someone had probably dobbed him in. Or maybe the police just waited here taking a punt. You heard of these arrests all the time. It was bad luck all right, but I couldn't do anything. The train shuddered.

There weren't many passengers. Three or four sailors at the far end, and an old couple across the aisle. We all nodded vaguely to each other and turned to peer at the landscape. I had *Dubliners* to read but it could wait. There'd be a bit more daylight yet. In a few minutes we were crawling through the shunting yards where I'd stood pouting all those years ago. By this time steam engines had almost vanished completely. I spotted a few retired ones already sinking in the morning glory. In decades to come, damp eyes would gaze at their splendour, but at that moment they looked bilious.

We passed the showgrounds. You couldn't see much. A naked ferris wheel poking up, otherwise just a brick wall covered in hasty comments. Soon a row of comfortable suburbs, then the hills. A scenic hamlet or two, quite separate from the edge of the city. No one had dared to join the dots back then. Billboards, waving children, bushfire warnings. Then it was too dark to see. Dim lights came on in the carriage. It was much too early to try and sleep. Or read. The sailors were caught up in a conversation. Sports talk I'd say, by the gestures. The old people were nodding already. Their crossword had slipped to the floor.

Bells at level crossings intrigued me for a while. I wondered why their pitch varied as the train ripped past. I didn't milk the subject. It didn't warrant an ulcer. Further out in the bush, stretches of track ran near the highway. There wasn't much traffic. A few semi trailers that overtook us easily. Wouldn't be a bad job I thought, truck driver. Screeching pop-eyed through the night, no one on your back. Dangerous of course, but that's half the fun.

I hadn't lost interest in My People. But I still hadn't met any. Not really. I'd seen a few here and there, but they hadn't been in good shape. They obviously slept out and I was shy about approaching them in my relatively swish condition. Okay, my jeans were torn, but torn according to the hippie ethic, nothing to do with destitution.

I dragged out my blanket and curled up. I didn't feel like reading *Dubliners*.

* * *

The old guy was coughing. Nothing alarming, obviously routine. I let the blind up. 'Fosters'. What's that? 'Four'n Twenty pies'. New trappings. Another world. A bloke in uniform came through reminding us to adjust our watches. Outside, there was rubbish everywhere, both sides of the track. There were industrial swamps, sooty factories, grime, smoke, haste, people walking muzzled greyhounds, people on bicycles. There were sirens. There was urgency and squalor. "Yes!" I thought I'd whispered, but the others looked across.

I bundled up my stuff and got near the door. Everyone did the same. They all talked at once. We were still twenty minutes out. I'd thought I was an authority on railway yards, but here I saw the real McCoy — Dodgem cars for grown folks. The near-miss club. A miraculous business. I hadn't tried to picture Melbourne, but I'd never have come up with this. I saw 'Spencer St. Station' in mammoth letters. It was official.

There was polite scrambling. The train, as I mentioned, hadn't been packed, but even so, this station was no Sleepy Hollow. No one dawdled. Everyone had somewhere to go. I hadn't thought much about where I'd stay. With sixty dollars, I figured *I'd* call the shots. Someone had mentioned the fleapits right here near the station. A last resort. I had a few addresses. Carlton. St. Kilda. Urban communes. It was pretty free and easy for a while back then. Skin colour was nothing. 'Us and Them' referred to anti-war stance, long hair, narcotic experience et cetera. Doors would be open... I was in no hurry. I decided to loiter for a while and soak things up. I got toast and coffee and took in the show.

The train had emptied and the station crowd was starting to thin out. A worried looking guy with glasses and a straggly beard sat at the next table. He seemed to be inspecting the people, like me, but more deliberately. He was obviously waiting for a certain passenger who hadn't shown. And now probably wouldn't.

He peered at me a couple of times. There'd never been a secret handshake or anything but Cool people spotted each other at once in those days. What was it, apart from a ragged appearance, which the police or anyone else could perhaps rustle up? A serene expression maybe. Ancient wisdom was big. Anyway, this guy had The Look, and I guess I did too, much as I tried to avoid such nonsense. The next time he stared, I picked up my rucksack and sat down at his table.

"Waiting for someone?" I didn't muck around.

"Sort of." He was still cagey.

"A friend?"

"Not exactly." I'd seen this before. Paranoia. Everyone knew the word now. I waited. He stared at me a bit more and then moved his saucer to reveal a small photo.

"Him," he whispered. It was the draft dodger they'd arrested at Adelaide Station the night before. I broke the news. He wasn't horrified, he'd never met the guy. But he shook his head in a 'not again' way. I kept quiet. He'd explain or he wouldn't. He lit a cigarette and leaned back. He seemed to relax a bit. "What do you think?" he flung out at last. "Should people have to fight in someone else's war for the crime of turning twenty on a particular day?"

"Well no, of course not."

"I'm Simon Mordecai," he announced, and kind of beamed. It was supposed to come across like Che Guevara, I think, but it meant less to me than Four'n Twenty pies.

"I've just come from Adelaide, Simon. It's my first time in Melbourne."

"Ah."

20

"My name's Wanda," I added. He picked up a fork and poked at his food. It was some kind of honey cake.

"Well, Wanda, I'm kind of an agent here, a people smuggler if you like. I help conscientious objectors to lay low. The powers know about me, and I've been apprehended several times, but legally it's a touchy area. I don't actually shelter them myself, and since I'm a private citizen, and not, for instance, an employer, I'm not obliged to ask my clients for papers. Consorting won't hold, because they're not criminals in the usual sense. The photos could prove awkward, but they never search me."

"Why do you carry the photos?"

"Don't ask. My visual memory is worth about twelve cents."

"How many blokes have you saved?"

"Not enough. Not nearly enough."

"How did *you* duck the call up? Luck of the draw?"

"Well, no. My number popped out, but I'm an asthmatic. Besides, how can they use Ray Charles? These specs aren't from the gag shop."

"What will you do now?"

"About Mr X? Nothing. 'Another man done gone.' I can't change that. Have you relocated to Melbourne? Where are you staying?"

"I don't know where I'm staying, but yeah, I've moved here."

"There's a vacant wing at my place." I stared at him. "I can offer you a room. It's a big house, you'd like it."

"How much is the rent?"

"For me, nothing. My great uncle left it to me. Pay what you can."

"Who else lives there?"

"No one. I'm the local weirdo. But not all *that* weird. I need twelve rooms? What for?"

"Why me?"

"I know you won't make trouble. I'm never wrong about people."

"I haven't got a job or anything."

"As I said, pay what you can. And when you can. I can afford to wait. Do I look undernourished? Don't answer. I'm no Atlas, I know that. What do you say?"

"Okay. Great. Thanks. I'll have a look anyway."

"Good. Is that the lot?" He nodded at the floor.

"One bag, yeah, that's it."

"Let's go then. I've probably got a parking ticket. They hound me all the time. Jay-walking they get me for. Sounds like a joke, right? But it's true. Do you know much about the Nazis? Ah, there it is, can you see a ticket? This car was Saul's too. My great uncle. It's a Mark IV Jag. He said they'd never top this model. He was right. It's about my age. Hop in. Don't worry, I can drive okay. A Swiss guy made these glasses. A genius. Friend of my father's. Relax. They'd soon grab my licence if there were any doubt."

Simon slid back the sun roof and we took off. I saw the cheap rooming houses. Sleazy they looked, not romantic at all. I started to appreciate my flukey luck. There was a lot of pointing at the car. People laughed, or else nodded like experts. Simon looked straight ahead. After a few minutes I couldn't resist. I jumped up and stuck my head and shoulders into the warm breeze. I waved at everyone.

"This is your Queen Mother routine, am I right? But please, Wanda, the cops." Fair enough. I flopped back in the seat.

"I'm puzzled, Simon."

"Let me guess. If I'm so worried about the police, why do I drive a collector's item? Why do I go to the station myself instead of sending an unknown? Adventure, that's why. Cloak and dagger. It's my pay-off. Was that your question?"

"More or less. Hey, what's that?"

"The M.C.G. Melbourne Cricket Ground, it's world famous."

"Have you been in there?"

"Yeah, a few times, to football games. My father gets a season ticket. Mainly for business friends."

"Is he a big wheel?"

"My father? He's a candyman. Literally. He makes chocolate, and sells it all over the country. Asia too. And New Zealand. Dolce Vita Confections. You've heard of it? How about Bliss Bars?"

"Bliss Bars? Is that you?"

"It's my father. I'm a shareholder. There's the mighty Yarra, what do you think? No one appreciates it. I do. I think it's stately. We used to paddle in it when we were kids. We lived at Kew. I wouldn't do it now, it's full of crap, but still…"

"Do you have brothers and sisters?"

"A sister in London. She's a lawyer."

"Where are we now?"

"We're nearly there, this is my patch. South Yarra it's called."

We drove up a hill and through a few backstreets. Everything looked pretty swish. Quiet. Leafy. Like in a picture book. Simon turned into a driveway and we entered a jungle.

"Now you can stick your head out. No, you'd better not, the branches need lopping, I never get round to it. You can be the gardener maybe. Only if you feel like it. Elbows in, this shed was built for a pony and trap. Yeah, climb out through the top. There's a proper garage that Uncle built, but it's full of junk. Well, not junk, blocks of stone, and sculpture tools. Friend from university. She's gone to America. Here we are."

We'd fought through the bushes. The joint was huge. One storey, but spread out. A creeper covered everything. Even the windows were in jeopardy. Simon unlocked the back door. He had to use his shoulder on it.

"It's worse in winter. I'm getting it fixed. Just drop your bag. We'll have coffee and I'll show you round. Do you want food? There's probably something."

Even the kitchen was vast. Cupboards right up to the ceiling. A marble sink that took up the length of a wall. An immense rusty furnace. A battered table maybe twelve feet long or more.

"Grab a chair. Milk? Sugar? No? I slurp coffee all day. I think I'm an addict. Let's see. There's dried fruit, bread, cheese. No? I'll cook something later. Why did you come to Melbourne? I can guess why you left Adelaide. I spent a couple of days there once. Mother was alive then and we all stayed at the South Australian. A wonderful hotel, but you walk out in the street and suddenly you know the face of angst. Ruth was there too, my sister. We were just children but you don't have to be Lawrence to recognize a desert. Father had business calls to make, and Mother took us for a walk round town. We went to a cafe. I remember crying my head off when I saw what passed for cakes. I was about eight. Ruth must have been ten. She didn't cry. She tried to make me eat some of her doughnut. Ruth's a showoff."

"What's that for, Simon?" A row of bells hung near the door. Numbered bells.

"How embarrassing. It's a relic from feudal times. Master would pull a cord and the lackeys jumped."

"Your uncle had servants?"

"No, no, Earlier Days. But I should get rid of it. Grab your coffee, we'll make the tour."

We crossed a kind of tiled foyer. I looked up at the dim skylight. Here too the ivy had progressed.

"Ah, the leaves. I should get up there soon. I'll show you the study first. Here we are. Uncle Saul's office. The bookroom. He was a genuine scholar. Any subject you like. Philosophy mainly. History, Theology, Psychology. Art History over there. A tight ship as you can see. Everything catalogued. What about this? Three, four, five shelves on Nazi Germany. He was obsessed. Who can blame him? He scrambled under fences to get out of Europe. Let's see. These are all Foreign Language, French, Latin... That wall's got novels. The right stuff too. He didn't harbour comic strips...and here's the famous Bosendorfer." Simon lifted the lid and plunked a note. A piano like this would have filled a normal-sized room.

"A luxury, I know, but Saul could play. Maybe not concert level, but not far off. He claimed to have known some of the legends personally. Horowicz, Rubenstein, the violinist Kreisler. We'll move on."

We took a different door out of the study into an even larger room. The banquet hall it would have been in 'feudal times'. Now it had a tennis table and a stereo set-up. And couches near the fireplace. "I don't give parties, but here's where they'd be...you get the idea."

Back through the foyer this time.

"This is my bedroom, nothing to see, a shambles. I'll tidy it up soon. Do you want another coffee? I'm having one. Back in a minute. Keep exploring, nothing's locked. Any of the other rooms you can have, take your pick."

Simon leapt off to the kitchen. Still half a dozen rooms or so. I'd checked out three of them when Simon found me again.

"What do you think? I'll show you the furnished one at the end. It's probably the best anyway, but you decide, we can move things around, that's no hassle."

He was right. I glanced in at others on the way. You couldn't call them weak links, but here at the far edge of the building was something special. It jutted out into the garden. It really was a kind of wing. Windows on three sides. Private bathroom.

"There you are, the Blue Room. Yes?"

"Yes. What can I say?"

Simon had picked up my bag. He tossed it into the corner.

"Welcome. I'll leave you to it. I've got a few calls to make. The phone's not bugged, I tell myself. Ha!" Simon bounded away, spilling coffee.

I distributed my property. Light work of course. I opened all the windows and sat on the bed. Had I really been in Adelaide sixteen hours ago? Haggling at the corner shop about dubious milk? Yes. Those were facts, and so was my new situation. This, I suppose, was the moment for suspicion, cynicism, perhaps even fear. But I'd leave that stuff for the tremblers of the world. They could form a tear-stained queue. And obligation? Guilt? I wouldn't walk into those traps either.

Simon had mentioned the overdue gardening in fun, but I'd do it anyway. There were months of work. Not cosmetic either. Houses can fall to bits under that kind of growth. It really was a jungle, I'm not exaggerating. I didn't plan devastation. No short back and sides. There'd still be dense terrain. But the spreading ivy was an emergency. And I'd clear a path or two.

I hopped out the end window onto a thick lawn, yellow at that time of year. A magnolia tree shaded most of it. From a low branch the remains of a swing dangled. Not Simon's. Certainly not Uncle Saul's. The rope looked to me like fifty years' worth. Ancient iron furniture sat near a crumbling fountain. There was no water. A stone flamingo hovered on its edge, one leg tucked up. There were bees everywhere, and cabbage moths. A metallic whir filled the air. Cicadas. They were new to me then. Crickets through an amp. I sprawled out in the shade.

* * *

Siesta's not my habit. It must have been the heat and the buzzing. When I came to, the whole lawn was in shadow, and traffic hummed close by. Five, maybe six o'clock. I crawled back in the window, showered, and dug out my red shirt and almost new overalls. Bib and brace they were, dyed yellow. I leapt down the passage to find Simon. He was in his room talking on the phone. I started whistling something. Simon wound up his patter and came out.

"Wanda. I knocked on your door earlier. Did you sleep?"

"Yeah, out on the lawn."

"My father phoned. He might drop in tonight on his way

27

to a conference. Flying visit he said, which could mean three hours or a couple of minutes. I told him you're here. You might find him alarming, I don't know."

"I haven't got any fancy clothes."

"Ah, you look okay. Do you want a drink? Uncle's cupboard's not bare yet. I'll dust off a red. I don't know what's there. Doesn't matter anyway, I wouldn't know the difference. What do you think?"

"Okay, if you like, thanks."

"The party room." Simon led the way and we dragged a couch over to the window. There was a bit of a breeze. He fished a bottle and glasses out of a wall closet and poured the wine. I'd been merry a couple of times on beer but claret was a new scene. It smelt pretty awful but I sipped at it. Simon put a record on.

"I've got a client to meet tomorrow morning, Wanda. He's from Perth, an airport job. That's rare. I guess because conscripts are usually poor. Anyway, I have to be out there by eleven. You might like to come for the spin. Got any plans?" I was about to mention my gardening program when the doorbell clanged. Simon whispered, "Father!" and skipped away, still clutching his drink. I heard footsteps and a loud voice. "What's this now? My son the shicker?"

"Of course not, Father. Just a glass of wine to welcome Wanda!"

"Ah! Wanda! Yes, show her to me."

A big guy with a beard stepped in holding Simon's arm. He didn't wait for introductions.

"So you're Wanda."

"Hello, Mr Mordecai."

"Gene, call me Gene. How do you like my son the

freedom fighter? What do you think of his cave?"

"This house? It's great. Very comfortable."

"Comfortable?! For Boris Karloff maybe. I keep telling him to sell and find something reasonable. A flat, a one man show. But no, no, Buckingham Palace he wants. With Uncle Saul — he's told you about Saul? With Saul it was different, he studied, he practised, a dozen bare rooms made sense. But for Simon. What's that on the gramophone? Elgar again. Swirling melodrama, that's what. You worry me Simon, but that's your role, you're my son. Why Elgar? Benny Goodman's not up to standard? Is that your idea? I get seasick even thinking of Elgar. Why don't you close the window? You're inviting the bats in now?"

"Please Father, you know there aren't any bats."

"And there are no snakes I suppose? I know about snakes, Wanda, I was bitten."

"Father."

"Let me tell. I was bitten. I forget the breed, quite dangerous. In Israel it was, seven, eight years ago. I was working in the fields. You should try working, Simon. I was working and received a nip on my finger, right there, you can still see. I ran over to the plough and cut it straight away on a sharp edge and sucked out the poison. They drove me to the doctor and rushed me into his rooms. Luckily I was able to describe the culprit, and a cure was at hand. But the doctor was angry. 'Shmuck! Vot for you cut?' I told him. Australian folklore. He wasn't buying. 'Ugh! Folklore! If you recover, get yourself a lottery ticket. Go now please. I have sane patients vaitink!'

"In Israel, everyone's an expert. It can be a little confusing sometimes. Here it's different. Everyone relaxes, awaits guidance. Here they read the newspapers right through, they watch ads on the television. Anyone with an ounce of spark will do well. You're smirking Wanda, you've noticed these things already, I can tell. Good. You'll succeed if you want to. Maybe you don't want to. That's alright too. Look, I must go. I'm parked in the street. Walk me there, Simon. You shouldn't have reminded me about the snakes. Goodnight Wanda, nice to meet you."

"Goodnight Mr Mordecai."

"Gene, call me Gene. Bring a cane Simon. Make noise! Make plenty of noise!"

They clattered out. I sat on the window sill and fumbled with the pushy creeper. Some of it was like rope. It meant business. There'd be a wrestling match but I'd win. I'd pay my way.

Simon came back in looking drained.

"Well, that's Pater. What do you think?"

"I thought he was fun."

"Fun? After twenty years you'd have a different angle. Contradiction, criticism, over and over. Doesn't matter what I do. He liked you though, he approved."

"What did he say?"

"Nothing. That's the point. Silence means nine out of ten at least. I've learnt that much. Even my childhood friends were monsters in Father's view. The most wide-eyed toddler would provide material for a lecture. Or a series of lectures. It's been the same ever since. Very few escape. Congratulations." Simon gulped his wine. "Refill, Wanda?"

"No thanks, I'm still going. You finish it."

"I think I will. Shicker he called me. Drunkard. Three drinks a year I take, maybe less. He *looks* for ways to insult me."

"He doesn't want you going to the dogs, Simon. That's all it is. Keep your shirt on. What was that about working in the fields in Israel?"

"Ah, lots of our friends do that. Six months or a year on a kibbutz. Communal farming. Various reasons. For Father it was discipline. And self-sufficiency appeals to him of course. I'll still be expected to do it sooner or later."

"Why don't you?"

"With my physique? Anyway, I'm too busy right now. Sure you don't want more of this?"

"No thanks. I thought I'd start on the jungle tomorrow."

"Pardon?"

"I'll start pruning the garden."

"What for?"

"I know you only mentioned it in passing but I'll do it. Someone has to, or you'll be strangled."

"Well, suit yourself. I don't remember what I say half the time. Did your parents torment you?"

"No, not really. They were foster parents, and a bit of a mystery to me. And I to them, probably." I told Simon what I knew, the only snippet I had of my cloudy origin. He listened but didn't answer. He looked cock-eyed after his three or four tumblers. Eventually he got up and started pacing between the stereo and the ping-pong court. I just watched. Up and down the room he went. Suddenly he realized the record had stopped, and flipped it over.

"You don't know him Wanda. If we'd been listening to Benny Goodman, he would have wanted a symphony. Anyway, stuff him. Let's have more swirling melodrama." Simon turned the music up and started waving his arms around. I was still perched on the window and he stared

31

right past me. I thought he was going to start conducting the cicadas, but he wasn't quite *that* Disney. His arrogance had vanished and left a pretty big gap. He sat down again and looked at the floor. I'd preferred him sober and loud.

"Shall we have coffee, Simon?" Bingo! he was half way back just at the sound of the word. He jumped up. His face showed relief, anticipation, even admiration. I felt like I'd invented the wheel. He strode to the kitchen grinning. He was an odd customer alright. The bouncing ball type. A minute later he came back in with a plate of shortbreads.

"My bourgeois streak," he muttered, and ran out to grab the whistling billy. We set up a picnic on the tennistable. He was suddenly in great shape, chuckling like a kid. He turned Elgar down a couple of notches and started talking.

"Forgive my passing horrors, Wanda. I shouldn't drink at all, that's obvious. You've seen Father at his best. You think I'm a brat. Ungrateful, unappreciative. Maybe you're right. But how can I live up to his pipe dreams? He scares me. He crosses my rhythm. He brings out the Clark Kent in me. I feel like the bumbling apprentice. He could send me out for pigeons' milk and I'd reach the door before the penny dropped. It's unnerving. Where you don't have power you have fear. I read that I think. Anyway, it's true. Father enters and the Muses roll over. My knees buckle.

"He did invite me to Israel, you know. My sister was away at a private college. Mother had died a year or so before and Father had been very quiet most of the time. It was a rough patch and he'd stopped treating me like a kid. 'Come to Israel, Simon. Just one year. We'll farm in the sun. We'll be human.' It sounded okay, sort of. I knew it would work for him, and that's what bothered me. I knew he'd labour like a maniac, he'd outstrip everyone, he'd emerge triumphant. And I'd be the wheezing punk, his burden. At fourteen you see all these possibilities and imagine a few others. You're strolling on a blade's edge, gambling on the breeze.

"I turned down his offer. At the time we had a lady with us who helped with the cleaning and so on. What's funny? Yeah, okay, we had a *servant*. Old Mrs Gulliver, a widow. I wanted to stay home with her and keep my life on its track. School, movies at the weekend, the odd game of chess with friends. Father wouldn't hear of it. If I didn't go to Israel, I'd enter Mr John Talbot's school for young men, as a boarder.

"My father wasn't taken in by Talbot's pamphlet or anything. The school was clearly a lunatic society, but Father saw this move as an airtight bluff. Unfortunately I called it, and for about ten seconds I felt victorious. Father's eyes popped out, but a deal's a deal.

'Are you sure, Simon?'

'Yes.' A reckless move. A week later we made an appointment. A couple of thugs took us round the place. Prefects. What did I think? I thought they were Nazis. Father probably did too, but we maintained our poker faces. 'It seems very clean,' we blurted out together. Here was the time to laugh and make a dash. But the moment passed. Would we like to meet Mr Talbot? Of course. Yes.

"This guy — this guy was cause for alarm. I knew he was only in his twenties but he'd spent a lot of time worrying. You could see that. Less than a year before, he'd won a major sports award. He'd also pocketed a Ph.D. in something to do with anatomy. He was an accomplished cellist and sang leads in light opera. Renaissance Man, right?

You'd think so. But things had gone bung. I've heard various theories over the years. Something about his mother. All sorts of ideas. Guess work. I saw him close up. He looked forty at least. He looked like Julius Caesar on that fateful day. Same lines on his face, same haircut. Same attitude, I suspected, but I shook hands anyway. Why gloss over it? Here was a maniac. Steely eyed and vicious. With his henchmen nearby, he could even outstare Father.

"Out of the blue he said, 'We welcome all creeds.' Ha! I could imagine why. Still I kept quiet. It was up to my father. Nothing doing. He glanced at me, that was all. The last exit, and I'd driven past. Out came the chequebook."

Simon pushed the biscuits across. "Help yourself Wanda, they're from Scotland. This Talbot character turned out to be exactly what I'd expected. I won't say worse, it wouldn't have any meaning. You couldn't even call it Law and Order. It was more like drawing straws. You'd get six of the best for passing a certain point at the wrong time, or because you were the eighth boy in the lunch queue, or because you weren't, that kind of thing. Ha! There was one concession for me and a couple of others because of our asthma. We didn't have to play cricket. In fact we weren't allowed to. Corpses would have been poor commerce... I quite liked cricket as it happened.

"Things weren't rosy, and then there was Xerxes. This is what Mr Talbot called his favourite weapon. 'As you know, boys, Xerxes was a strong Greek ruler, ha ha ha.' Humour, you see. Did I raise my hand? 'Please Sir, Xerxes was in fact Persian.'

"No chance. If I'd reached *that* point, I'd have used cyanide, or gas. Or a school tie maybe. Anyway, this Xerxes had a steel edge. First you'd have to bend over at right angles and put your head under a desk. Then Mr Talbot would hack at your backside. 'Come out the front, Isaacs, we're going to slice bacon.' Thick cuts or thin, which hurt more? This debate raged on among the victims. Both are indescribable! Plus of course you banged your head on the desk when you leapt up. A reflex. No one ever stayed put when Xerxes made contact.

"Talbot's method, that's how it went. It's produced a few bigshots, if you count the underworld. Also mental patients, a startling proportion. How did I get onto this? That's right, me and Father. Father and me. Luckily he came back from Israel after eight months, to sort out some business hitch. He bailed me out. I hadn't even been able to write letters. No one could. It was a rule.

"I know Father felt bad about his stubbornness. He shouldn't have put me in there. But then, I'd only had to say okay to the trip. The next few months weren't bad. We didn't argue much. Father was quite fit from the manual work in Israel. Plus he had his snake bite saga to hawk around. After a year though, it was back to cat and dog, or mouse, or whatever it is. I'm getting tired. Is that coffee still hot? Warm, that'll do."

"What happened to this Talbot? You can't get away with that stuff can you?"

"Apparently you can. Well, sort of. The school eventually closed down, but only because the word got round. There was never any criminal prosecution or anything like that. Talbot himself is still a semi-public figure. He's some kind of coach at a football club. Not the big league, but he does okay. He owns a gym too. Flash Jack's Workout or something. It's in St Kilda I think. I needn't point out that I've never been there. I must admit that I still consider revenge. An exposé of some sort. I've asked my father to use his influence, but he thinks I'm being petty. He's never interested in vengeance. Father's a steamroller in his way, but scandal and back-stabbing don't suit his ethics. You think that's admirable? You could be right, but you didn't have to meet Xerxes."

Simon rambled like this for another couple of hours, maybe longer. I got the impression he'd never had a proper audience before. Not for a long time anyway. Here was his poor heart, throbbing away on a tattered sleeve. I learnt a great deal. I'd never thought of Easy Street as having pot-holes. Now and again he hopped up to boil coffee. Sometimes he just stared blankly for several minutes, wading in his nightmares. We scoffed all the shortbreads and a few dried figs. It was enough. At about ten, Simon stuck another record on. Hillbilly music this time. The very-sad-indeed variety. He stared at the wall a bit more. He was miles away. I said goodnight but I don't think he heard. I couldn't find the switch in the passage and had to grope along the wall. In my room I flopped down straight away. The door had a latch but I knew I wouldn't need to use it.

* * *

Birds woke me. Screeching lorikeets. An elegant clock stood on the mantelpiece but I hadn't thought to wind it. Six thirty or seven was my guess. It was hot again. No excuse. It was a work day. I found my torn-at-the-knees jeans, rock'n'roll trousers. And my worst T-shirt. I stuck my head under the cold tap. Bits of Simon's blues still rang in my ears. I went to the party room and gathered up the cups and things. Simon's door was half open and I heard his snores. I found a coke in the fridge and skulled it with rye bread and jam.

Outside in the yard I could hear the traffic noise starting to build. There was Simon's Jag wedged into the old stable. Further along the house wall, I noticed an ivy clad ladder, a fixture. I climbed up it and found a concrete deck with a canvas chair on it. From this point, I had a pigeon's angle on the whole scene. I saw the top of the magnolia. Gables blocked my view of the part where I'd snoozed the day before, but everything else was clear from up there. The bigger trees made patterns. Avenues, arcs, stuff like that. Must have been geometric in its day. Now it was Rafferty's rules. It looked great. I wouldn't tamper with most of it, but the house had to be rescued. Ivy duty. That was the mission. Endless work of course, I'd never catch up. So what. Better than having a wall tilt five inches a year. I spotted a tin shed among the lantana bushes. Full of tools no doubt. I got down the ladder and headed for the spot.

Sure enough, hoes, rakes, hacksaws. Bicycles too, from another age. Rusty of course, wrinkled tyres. I found a tomahawk with a passable edge and headed for the most urgent job. Outside the party room it was. The stuff had grown claws, it was out-running the snails. At first the blade bounced straight off. I practised on thinner parts until I figured out the tricks. After a while I made a few dents. Peak hour noise had grown and faded again. Did that make it nine o'clock? Later? Two or three hours to retard one branch? It was madness. But the immediate option was to be a freeloader, running up an unpayable debt. No option really. Otherwise I'd have to get money somehow and rent my room properly. But how?

Over the next hour or whatever it was, nothing changed, certainly not the ivy. Then I heard the car start up. I dashed around the corner to greet Simon. I climbed up and looked through the sunroof. He was tapping at his watch. But the Jag had to idle for at least a minute. You don't whip thoroughbreds.

"Simon."

"Hah! You scared me. It's after ten, I forgot to set the alarm. What are you doing with that thing?"

"Scratching at the creeper. I told you I would. Will you make the airport in time?"

"I hope so. If the traffic's thin. Look, hop down, I'm taking off. See you about one if you're here."

"I'll be here."

He reversed out and disappeared between the elms. I returned to my task. I shouldn't have stopped at all. The ivy branch had grown back again, I was sure of it. But I kept hacking anyway. Blisters had appeared and my shoulder and neck ached. I tried it left handed. Slower still, of course. I was thinking about going inside for a drink when I heard the back door bell. Could be anyone. The police even. I stayed put. My presence would be hard to explain. My People didn't camp on this real estate. But I had to peep. I crawled under the rain water tank and parted the leaves. Simon's father was back.

"Mr Mordecai!"

"Is that Wanda? Where are you? Ah!" He'd found me. I beat my way through and stood up. "Simon's gone out. To the airport."

"Ah yes, the Kamikaze Kid. Never mind, it's you I want to speak to."

"Me?" Trouble, for sure.

"Yes. Look at you! What have you been doing?"

"I was gardening. Cutting back the ivy."

"Ha! Without a bulldozer? You're even more ambitious than I thought. We must talk. Where can we sit? Let's go inside." The party room again. Mr Mordecai took the couch near the window. No bats at this hour. I stood near the mantelpiece.

"Can I get you coffee? Or a cold drink?"

"No. No thanks Wanda. I have a proposition for you."

I couldn't believe it. Simon's father trying to haul me into his bunk? To him I was brown sugar. So much for his famous ethics. How embarrassing. A middle aged gent. But no, I was miles off target.

"When I left here last night, Wanda, I attended a board meeting. I believe Simon's told you about our company? Yes? Well, much was discussed. Expansion and so on. I won't go into that. But also our next advertising program. This part concerns you."

"Me? How?"

"I take it you don't have a job."

"Not yet. I mean, I'm helping with the garden here. I'm not a bum, Mr Mordecai."

"No, no, of course not, or I wouldn't be talking to you. But you don't have an income, right?"

"Not yet, no."

"How can I put this... If you think I'm insulting you, or making fun, or any such thing, say so at once and I'll leave. I need your face for a promotion. A Chocolate Girl."

"Chocolate girl? You mean Aunty Tom?"

"Ha! ha! Alright, forget I spoke. You — "

"No, I'm still curious. What would I have to do? Melt Bliss Bars under my straw hat?" This doubled him up. He roared. He was almost hysterical. He pulled at his beard. He kicked his shoes off. A laughing tycoon is spectacular.

"Wanda, let's be serious about this." He had the giggles, not me. "Wanda, listen." He found his shoes. "I haven't mentioned the idea to anyone else. I usually leave these matters to the ad people, but they'd never have conceived this. I want a laughing girl, *you* in fact, to appear on posters and billboards. You wouldn't have to nurse the product, or do anything zany. You'd be a symbol of Australia, that's all. It's about time this country stopped cringing."

"So I'd be a trade mark?"

"Not a trade mark exactly, but an emblem. In foreign countries especially we need such an image. But here too, why not? You'd work perhaps half a day in front of the camera. Five hundred dollars. Television later, if it fires. What's your response?"

My turn to laugh. Five hundred dollars. My father wouldn't make that in two months. But I didn't laugh. I was bewildered. Not about the pay of course. If I'd wanted the job, even fifty dollars would have seemed like a pot of gold. But what was at stake? Did it degrade my race even further? Or did it do the opposite? And did I want to part with my privacy before I'd started to live? My colour alone drew too much attention for my liking. Fame wouldn't help at all. Besides, it would be unearned fame. Blinking at a lens is no great achievement. On the other hand...

"Can I tell you tomorrow, Mr Mordecai?"

"Of course, of course. You can have a month if you need it, but no more. We'll have to get on to it then. Say four weeks from today. Here's my card, my work number. Phone me when you've decided. And, a small favour —

secrecy, yes? It's probably lucky that Simon's out, he talks a little. See you soon."

I steered him to the door and he marched off through the wilderness. He was preoccupied. He'd forgotten about the snake question.

* * *

I'd left Adelaide to chase action. There'd been plenty in two days. Now a pay cheque too if I wanted it. Five hundred dollars had a better ring to it than Ivy Duty. But, like I said, it was a dilemma. I didn't return to the gardening straight away. It could have easily triggered a hasty decision. I'd be loitering at the crossroads for a month. The easy part. But eventually the hour of decision would come around. I could flip a coin, but I preferred reason. I figured a stroll through the rest of the garden might help. I decided to try and find the other shed, the 'proper garage' that Simon had said was full of sculpture, or something. I hadn't seen it from the fountain area near my room. Nor from the rooftop. No doubt it was over-grown, like everything else.

I meandered through the weeds. There were shrubs and bushes like I'd never seen before. I found a small glass-house bursting with neglected exotica. And I found the garage. The door from the yard was unlocked. In one corner was a hoist thing with a grubby engine rusting at its base. From the Jag maybe. There were step ladders. There was a dusty bench with a tool board on the wall above it. Chisels mainly. A couple of mallets. And elsewhere large objects under covers. I stripped one of them. A block of stone with crosses and half moons all over it. Meticulous

41

work but meaningless to me. I flung the sheet back over and tried another.

Ah! Blank eyes glared down from a gigantic woman. Eight feet tall at least. Impressive. A long face with sharp angles. Maybe she wasn't even finished. I'm no art critic. But she was a class act alright. I checked the other three figures. All embryonic. Mapped out in pencil, but not started. Like the first one. I peered at the stone woman for a while longer. Then I put the covers back and went out. In those few minutes clouds had crept up. It was still hot, but rain seemed likely. I shut the garage and found my way back to the house.

It was still a bit early to expect Simon. I went to my room and showered. My aches persisted but I felt sharp again in my yellow overalls. The gardening clobber I'd chucked into a corner. Had I decided already to be the Chocolate Girl? No. Not yet. I had a month and I'd use it. I wouldn't mention Mr Mordecai's visit at all. I didn't want to be forced into lying. I sat on the bed and tried to weigh up the situation, and sort out the moral side, if there was one. Not easy for a country cousin. I'd heard of the bright lights trap. I'd heard of fools' gold. They looked different close up. I made no progress.

My maze of thoughts was disrupted by a knock on the door.

"Wanda." Simon's voice. I opened up.

"Wanda, I'd like you to meet Wayne Turbill. He's from Perth."

This guy was evil. I'm not the jumpy type but here we had a bona fide ice block. Blonde moustache and thin straight hair. You can't have yellow eyes. I'll call them green.

42

"Hi Wayne." His mouth moved I think.

"I've invited Wayne to stay with us tonight, Wanda. I forgot to consult my addresses before I dashed off this morning. No billet, no mission. I'll sort it out tomorrow. It was pretty sticky, approaching Wayne in public. It's all cool though."

Simon turned to his guest. "Plenty of floor space my friend, but no beds. There's a couch."

"Whatever." Wayne's mouth definitely moved.

"I'll show you the bathroom, Wayne. See you later on, Wanda." Off they went. What was Simon thinking of, bringing his dodgers here? Even pacifists and hippies could cause him trouble, indirectly. But this Wayne? Who was he? Did Simon *want* to get caught? Mr Mordecai's tough attitude with his son started to make sense to me. Someone had to shake him up, preferably this side of prison.

I couldn't even think with Wayne in the house. I jumped through my window to prowl around the garden again. I had trouble getting that jackal's face out of my head. I tried to fix the old swing. I scraped built-up mud out of the fountain. I circled the house a couple of times, and sat in the car for a while. I hacked at the ivy. The rain finally showed up and I ran to the sculptor's shed. The studio. I flicked on the light and unveiled my mate. It felt okay out there with the statue. I stayed as long as the rain lasted. Hours maybe. I thought about the Chocolate Girl, and about Wayne and Simon. Nothing was clear. When the showers eased up I went back to my room, via the window. I pulled the blind down and locked the door. It was cooler now after the rain. I found an extra blanket in the wardrobe and hopped into bed. It was still daytime, only about four, probably.

It was dark when Simon called out and woke me. "Do you want to eat, Wanda? Wayne's gone down to get something. He should be back any minute."

"Hang on." I unbolted the door.

"Why are you locked in? Don't you trust me?"

"Because of Wayne. He's lethal."

"Wayne's my client. Okay, a rough diamond. I can't pick and choose. He'll be gone tomorrow anyway."

"For how long?"

"How would I know? Till the war ends. He'll lay low in the house where I send him. Lilydale as it happens, way up in the hills. We won't see him again. Relax. Just one night. I could have sent him there today I suppose, but it's a bit late now, it's after nine."

"This is more of your cloak and dagger, isn't it Simon? Your pointless danger thing, having him at your house?"

"I don't know. Yeah, maybe. Do you want any food?"

"No thanks, I don't think so. What have you been discussing with him?"

"The draft mainly. He's arranged for a few of his friends to contact me. They're coming over in about three weeks in separate cars. He needs addresses."

"Have you given him any?"

"No, why?"

"Send him to a non-existent number. Do anything. Unless you want to share a cell with your Lilydale colleague."

"That's crazy, Wanda. Wayne trusts me, I can't do that. I'd never — Ah, he's back. You sure you won't come out?"

"I'm sure. What have you told him about me?"

"Nothing."

"Good. He probably assumes I'm your maid. Let's leave it like that."

44

"Wanda…"

"He's calling out. Go. I don't want him near me."

"Okay, okay. I'll see you tomorrow."

"Think, Simon. Think."

* * *

The sun had made good progress by the time I woke up. No sign of rain, and the heat was returning. I decided to skip Ivy Duty, but not because of the weather. I had to sort out this Wayne thing. There was silence. I went to the kitchen. There was a note from Simon near the coffee jar. "Have taken W to L." Great. He'd turned cabby. Why didn't he just drive the Mark IV up the steps of Police Headquarters? With a few balloons, he could make a day of it.

Simon had left his watch as a paper weight. Afternoon already. I'd slept fifteen hours, a record. The flip side of hard labour. Would I see my friend Simon again? Through iron bars maybe, with a twitching goon at my elbow. Right now though, I could only wait. I paced all over the house, the study, all the vacant areas. Not Simon's room. I went out to the gate. I peered up and down the street. I craned my neck like a war bride. It was all a novelty, but not much fun. I headed back to the kitchen and checked Simon's watch. I went to my room and wound up the clock and set it. This was the end of my creativity. I sat on the window sill and tried to imagine a vacuum. It was easy. I thought of the holy men in the Himalayas. They sit like this for thirty years or more. Their nails grow through their hands. They wait for people to buy them rice. They're mistaken for teachers.

I expected Simon to phone any time. From prison. I'd have to find his toothbrush and a carton of cigarettes. Maybe something for him to read. I jumped down onto the lawn and took the long way to the gate. At the house end of the driveway I spotted a new beer bottle. I kicked it along the avenue. I heard crunching gravel. Suddenly I was side-stepping the famous Mark IV headlights.

"Simon!" He skidded into the nettles. I jumped up on the bonnet.

"Why are you shouting? What's happened?"

"Nothing. You've still got your beard and your own clothes!"

"What are you talking about?"

"You know what I'm talking about. I thought Wayne would have you handcuffed by now."

"You're raving again. I drove him to Lilydale, gave him the address, left him on a corner."

"So discreet. I still think I'm right."

"How can you be right? I am here aren't I? Let me park the car. Hold tight."

"I'll walk."

I met him in the kitchen. "Do you want coffee, Simon?"

"Incessantly. Why are you so worried?"

"Wayne's setting you up for the jackpot. Did you give him those other addresses? For his friends?"

"Not yet. He'll be in touch."

"I bet he will."

"Relax. If anything dodgy comes up, I'll deal with it then."

"Oh yeah. With your one permitted phone call?"

"Forget it. Let's talk about something else." Not a bad idea.

"I snooped around in the other shed, Simon. Have you seen that statue?"

"Hm? Oh, Shelley's workshop. No, I haven't been out there for ages."

"When did she go to America?"

"Oh...six months ago. Last winter. I should write."

"You know where she is?"

"Of course."

"Could I write to her?"

"To a stranger? What for?"

"I don't know. I liked the statue. Can you give me her address?"

"I suppose so. Why not?" Simon flipped through his notebook. The straight one. His list of upright citizens. He handed over a loose slip of paper.

"Say hello from me. She knows I'm slack with letters."

"Is she your lover? What's the story?"

"Nah. A teenage thing. Now we're friends. Write to her. She'll like it."

"Is she taken seriously? Her work? Is that why she went to...what is it, Oakland?"

"No, no. The chipping bit's a sideline. She's mainly a musician, a singer."

"Is she good? I mean, you know, professional?"

"Yeah, she's magic. She knows a guy over there, a composer. They're planning to close in on the big time when they've got enough songs."

"Is Oakland big time? I've never heard of it."

"San Francisco is. It's next door."

"Do you think she'll answer my letter?"

"How would I know? Run the experiment. Write to her."

"Are you angry, Simon? You sound abrupt."

"No, no. Not angry. You've got me doubting Wayne."

"Good. Self-preservation, lesson one."

"You don't trust anyone, do you Wanda?"

"Yes I do. I trust you, for instance. And I trust myself. When my hair stands up, I look for a cause. In this case my gaze came to rest on Wayne's motives."

"Just let me consider it."

"I think I'll write to Shelley straight away. Are you going out again?"

"Yeah. I've got a couple of guys to meet at a pub. Twins they are. Their birthday marble rolled down the chute."

"At a pub? Why not the station?"

"Locals. The parents lost their nerve. What could they have done anyway? 'Please Mister, they is nice boys?' Sure. I'll be leaving in just over an hour. Do you want to go?"

"No, I don't think so. I'll stay in the shadows. It may come in handy if there's trouble."

In my room I found paper and envelopes. Even stamps. Even a typewriter, if I needed it. Endless manna from heaven. Or somewhere. I couldn't whinge. Wayne was the only fly in the ointment. He was hefty though.

"Dear Shelley..." Hmm. Easy enough to talk about it. Who was Shelley? I hadn't even seen a photo. Would that have helped? Probably not. My vote of confidence fluttered around the statue, nothing else. Well, I knew she was a singer. I could promise to buy all her records. Not quite my intended tone... Eventually I wrote half a page about her sculpture, exhausting my rustic vocab. And I got a bit reckless. Did she need some lyrics to glue onto her composer friend's tunes? If so, we could make a deal.

'I'm a poet, you see, Shelley.' That's what I said. I was stuck. I was tongue-tied. I couldn't leave it blank. It got worse. 'Your disciple, Wanda' I put at the bottom. And 'P.S. Hello from Simon.' Kidstuff. To make sure, I used about seven stamps. Simon laughed when he took it with him to post.

After these first two or three days, this blood-curdling overture, where could affairs move but into a slump? Wayne still crept in and out of my thoughts but I didn't mention his name. I'd let Simon's own meditation fertilize his doubts. The Chocolate Girl didn't vanish either. I'd made no decision. If I were to accept, then I was living on justified credit and therefore honourably. If not, then I'd have to plan something else. I picked at the creeper off and on, but could only regard the work as a token. I'd contributed a few bucks for groceries, but this too seemed like a feeble gesture. I'd slip into leechhood if I didn't watch out. I lost no sleep, but my days were prickly beneath their courtly facade.

One afternoon, the phone rang while Simon was out. This hadn't happened before. In fact it hardly ever rang at all. I thought it might be Mr Mordecai. Not that I had a yes or no to his offer. There were two weeks left to the deadline. I went into Simon's room and answered.

"Who's that? Is Simon there?" Wayne for sure. I hadn't heard much of his voice before, but I was certain.

"He'll be home around eight, can I take a message?"

"Who are you?"

"Wanda."

"Oh, you're the — We met briefly, you probably don't remember. Wayne Turbill."

"Yes I remember. Simon's mate from Perth. How are you?"

"I'm good. Listen, do you know how to write?"

"If you talk slow."

"Okay. Tell him I'll bring my friends to the Cricketers' Arms Hotel at nine thirty tonight. Have you got that? Cricketers' Arms, Richmond, just over the river. He'll know what it's about."

"I'll tell him."

"Good. Don't forget. It's very important for Simon to be there."

"Goodnight, Mr Wayne. I'll tell him." I hung up abruptly, like a greenhorn. Simon wouldn't be home till midnight at least. He'd made that clear. I checked his wall map of the city and inner suburbs. He'd love to jam coloured pins in it, I thought. And little flags. But he wasn't *that* careless. I found our street. I looked up the Cricketers' Arms in the phone book and stuck a mental flag there too. I had no idea of the map's scale, but the MCG was marked and the pub was slightly closer. Walking distance. It would be my first Melbourne jaunt. So far, the gods had been making house calls. I had a strong urge to go out at once, to make sure I could find this joint. Risky though. A squad car might pull up. Name? Address? Who else lives there? Messy. I'd just have to fidget for three or four hours, till it got dark.

Shelley's sculpture still intrigued me, but twice already that day I'd checked out the studio. I'd watered plants, and cut back the branches along the driveway. They'd been swiping at the car lately. I was ready for a new stunt alright, but another few hours wouldn't hurt. I went to the study and glanced at a couple of art books. I was too edgy to read properly. When the light started to fail I went to my room and climbed once more into my sweaty garden wear. Looking like a wino attracts a certain kind of attention it's true, but no one associates you with politics, or whatever it was I was about to dabble in. I sauntered out with Simon's binoculars under my shirt. I had a rough diagram, which I threw away at Punt Road. From here it was just over the river, like the man had said. The terrible Wayne.

I stopped on the bridge to look at the lights gleaming in the Yarra. A few cars honked at me. Harmless. They couldn't pull up here. Even police would baulk at that prospect. When I reached the other side it was all park. We must have driven along here from the station, but I hadn't noticed details then. Now I strolled easily in the darkness. There was a railway bridge and a bit of an intersection, then more greenery. Then the Cricketers' Arms, right opposite me. Luck and fate had teamed up again. It was easy. I had an hour or more to wait but that was okay. I couldn't draw too close, I couldn't peer in at the door. I could only witness comings and goings.

There was a negotiable tree and I scrambled up it. Uncalled for, of course. A Simonism. I swung my feet and looked through the binoculars. Nothing to report. Traffic flow medium to heavy. Two mature drunks shook their fingers at each other. Then they patched it up and disappeared in a side street. A guy with a crew cut came out with a paper bag. Estimated contents, two beers. None of my business. Immaterial. He waved down a cab. It stopped suddenly, picked him up, muscled back into the honking stream. Nothing at all for twenty minutes. Two laughing girls entered the premises. About my age. Caucasian. Then a further quiet patch. Then another taxi. It escaped the crush, squealing into the street beside the pub. It pulled up and Wayne got out. He was wearing a headband and a vinyl jacket with badges on it. He looked at his watch and went inside the bar.

I didn't know the time. Between eight thirty and nine I guessed. Here was Wayne outside again. He looked up and down the footpath. A good sign. He was early. Headlights were the only illumination, but they weren't scarce. Wayne lit a smoke. He tried to stroll casually up and down. It didn't suit him. He was ungainly. Suddenly he stopped shuffling and threw down his cigarette. He seemed to be staring across the road. Had he spotted me? No. He was looking at a Kombi Van that had pulled up on the footpath. My side. The northbound traffic was steady. Five shapes got out of the van into the obliging beams. Five robust males of bohemian appearance.

Over the road, Wayne took his headband off, wiped his forehead, went back into the Cricketers' Arms. The five, of course, looked both ways and crossed. I dropped down onto the grass. Okay, their Band of Stooges plot would fizzle. But they still had Simon if they wanted him. He'd sheltered a draft dodger, or thought he had. Offering Wayne a bed was probably worth a few months, or a year, in Pentridge. They'd cut their losses. They'd have his house surrounded by eleven. That was my guess.

How could I find Simon? He was somewhere out on a mission. Or perhaps he wasn't. I knew nothing. I'd have to ring his father. I should have known the office number by now. I'd pulled out the card often enough. I wasn't sure though. Fingers crossed for a phone book. And would he work this late?

I sprinted across the park. A dim phone box loomed. There were yellow pages. I found the number and dialed. A lady answered. A cleaner it turned out. "Mr Mordecai?" she gasped.

"Yes! Mr Mordecai. An emergency. It's about his son."

"He has a son?"

"Yes, please hurry, is he there?"

"He was before. Please wait. I look." I heard timid calling and door-knocking. Then someone running to the phone.

"Hello! Who's this?"

"Simon! What are you doing there?"

"Looking at the figures. I check them monthly. Don't forget, I'll own this outfit eventually. What's going on? I thought someone had borne me a son, I was racking my brain."

"Simon, you're in trouble. Leave your car wherever it is and get a cab. I'll meet you... I don't even know where I am. Make it the MCG... I don't know, the street side. Just stay in one spot. Get there now!" I hung up. I didn't feel like an argument. I took off back through the park. Another marathon. The MCG slowly grew... What a joint. You could run the Olympics in there. Maybe they had, in '56. What would I know? I'm down from the bush.

Part 2

Wet roads, and tramlines everywhere. They were the main traps. You had to stay on the ball to pedal a bike in Melbourne. I'd got one at a junk shop for twelve bucks. Nothing fancy, but it worked. No velvet gears or anything. From the same firm I'd got a three dollar overcoat. A bit kitsch. I'd found a beanie too, on a train. Blue and white. 'CATS' it said on the front. In Melbourne you take winter seriously. I was an expert by this time. It was late June 1970. I'd been living in Fitzroy for a month.

I stayed at Simon's place alone after he made his escape. He'd got away to Sydney okay. Mr Mordecai had set it up with one of his overnight couriers. He sent money to him the same way. Cash of course. About six hundred a month. Quite a lot back then. His dividends would cover it. They'd sort it out later. Simon could easily have got false I.D. and lounged on the north shore. But he didn't. He used an alias, but didn't bother with papers. Instead he crouched day and night in a no questions boarding house in The Rocks area. He'd dyed his beard and hair gray and played records all day. Swing era mostly. Even Benny Goodman perhaps. Who knows? He kept a bottle of White Horse that never left the drawer. The vicious Wayne and everyone else had probably forgotten all about him. But Simon didn't dwell on that bit. He was a Fugitive.

I gathered all this on the dripfeed. Simon wrote maybe every six weeks or so on average. Pretty good for him. Wanted folks have time to spare I guess. To receive his letters, I also needed a fake name and a c/o. Mr Mordecai arranged that too, with someone at the factory. He must have forked out plenty in tips. Hush money or whatever you call it. He wanted to make sure though. 'My son the jailbird' was unthinkable.

Mr Mordecai had insisted that I stay at the South Yarra house and keep an eye on things. I'd tried to get out of it. It seemed like squatting to me. We talked it over a lot the first few days after Simon left. He convinced me I'd be doing him a favour. He'd rather have me there than hire a security service. How much a week would I need to live?

"I can't take money as well, Mr Mordecai."

"How much?"

"I don't know. Fifteen dollars or something. I'd cut back the ivy though."

"The ivy! In other respects you're quite sane. The ivy shall be done. I'll send someone with a chainsaw. Yes, I know. He won't be a butcher. Relax. You'll look after Simon's house. You know what I think of the place. But it's his choice. You won't let him down, will you, Wanda?"

He could easily have dredged up the Chocolate Girl. But I guess that would have struck him as a shabby move. There was still about a week to go according to our agreement. Not a word. Gene Mordecai was an old type gent. You don't see that stuff any more. It's equated with mughood these days. I accepted the caretaker deal. I kept the house slick and the garden under control. Later I even did a bit of transplanting, and attempted a couple of trick shots, grafting and so on. Uncle Saul's library had a few books on horticulture. Some of them uncut. I guess his life had been flat out without these details.

I'd phoned Mr Mordecai on the agreed date about the Chocolate Girl. I'd told him thankyou, no, my taste for privacy had got the upper hand, and so on. He hadn't laughed at me, or tried to re-sell the idea. He'd understood. It was okay. I wonder whether Chocolate Girl would have got away with it in 1968? Dolce Vita Confections may have been a laughing stock. On the other hand, Mr Mordecai may have been hailed as a pioneer, an advertising genius. His competitors may have slapped their foreheads. "How did Gene think of that? The guy must have a crystal ball." Et cetera. Who knows? No understudy appeared. There was never a Chocolate Girl.

The night of the Cricketers' Arms caper, I'd stayed out late, tracking Mr Mordecai, arranging Simon's flight. Sure enough, Wayne's army was crouching there in the Kombi when I got home. I stuck to my pinhead approach.

"I don't know, Mr Wayne. I did tell him. The River's Arm, right?" He slapped me around a bit, but finally stormed off. They didn't even ask me where I'd been till four a.m. Black people go walkabout, everyone knows that. I spotted their van in the street a couple more times, but I wasn't seen. Nor was Simon of course. Nor the Jag. Mr Mordecai had taken care of business. His own apartment was searched, but that seemed to be the epilogue.

A month or so after I'd first written to Shelley, a brief thankyou note turned up. A few lines on a Golden Gate postcard. From her tactful condescension I realised that I had come across as a twelve-year-old, or thereabouts. Pretty much as I'd feared, back when my fan letter was crossing the waves. I tried again, with more thought. I may as well own up. I dug out a dictionary and skylarked a bit. Shelley's first impression had to be wiped out. This time I enclosed a snapshot taken in a booth, one of those coin-op things. Fingers crossed, I dropped the letter in the slot. Who knows what she made of my rapid progress, but anyway, she answered. On three or four pages. After that our writing was regular, and frequent. She was living with a bloke called Lloyd Moss, the composer that Simon had mentioned. She sent photos, coloured ones.

She and Lloyd both had long red hair. Lloyd played guitar and a bit of flute. Pretty slick, I gathered from Shelley's descriptions. They played two or three times a week, but for peanuts. They weren't the only ones chasing a recording deal, but they were confident. Shelley said they were 'rounding third'. I figured out what she meant from the rest of the letter. She meant they'd be famous next week at the latest. It didn't work out like this. When one of their home-made tapes arrived I realized why.

Lloyd's guitar playing was breath-taking. Tough and subtle at the same time. And Shelley was a nightingale, no two ways about it. But Lloyd's lyrics. Hmm. His tunes? Great! Schubert would have snaffled them. But you need more than melody to sell "I'd work at General Motors for you baby, yes I would, yes I would". I didn't comment. I said she and Lloyd sounded good together, and left it at that. But after a polite pause, two or three weeks, I started sending Shelley my own stanzas — like I'd hinted in my first embarrassing letter.

She liked them. Lloyd did too, but he wouldn't use them. He insisted on artistic control. I could imagine them on skid row. Two vast talents passing a paper bag. I was angry at Lloyd but kept it under my hat. I just continued to send lyrics. I didn't call them lyrics though. Here's another poem I'd say. A poem with chorus and bridge.

One day a psychedelic envelope showed up. Shelley had painted stars and rainbows and things all over it. Obviously big news. I thought maybe they'd landed a contract after all. But it wasn't that. Shelley was pregnant. It had been accidental, but she was really pleased. So was Lloyd. The possible effect on their career wasn't mentioned. They were going with the flow I guess. She said they would get married at the end of the year. Not because of the kid. Something about a work permit. She didn't go into detail.

They kept performing as a duo for about five months. Shelley took a break from the stage in February of '69. The wedding had been on New Year's Day. Lloyd kept playing solo for a while, but he wasn't a singer, and work was harder to find. He did radio jingles to survive. They kept sending their demo tapes to record companies. Most didn't reply at all. Some took the trouble to return the tape with a Dear John. They weren't always tactful. "Find a lyricist" was the general drift.

Lloyd wasn't a complete fool. Eventually my words found their way onto his manuscript paper. New tapes were made and sent to the appropriate string pullers. And to me. I felt like I'd scrambled up Everest. But with Shelley unavailable for live performance, things were tricky. There'd almost certainly be a recording contract, but not at present. That was okay. They'd been patient before and so had I. We were all going with the flow. The child appeared in June. A girl. They toyed with the name Wanda in salute of their pen pal, but in the end it was Mexico. Mexico Moss. Not bad.

* * *

Writing letters and sniffing at the winter roses. Who did I think I was? Some kind of hot-shot? A retired opera singer? It was crazy. It was time for a proper look at Uncle's library. Back in Adelaide I'd always been reading something. But hardly at all here. Strange. Too much available at once, I guess.

Simon had assured me there was no rubbish on the shelves. Good. I'd wasted enough time, one way and another. I had no method, no sort of general outline. I'd be plucking out novels like cards at a magic show. But I had to start somewhere. I decided to go by the covers, the magnetism of the titles: *Lost Illusions... Seize the Day... The Outsider... Hunger... The Magic Mountain...*

These and others grabbed my attention straight off. I took down *Seize the Day*. Saul Bellow. Was that Uncle Saul? Nah. Simon would have mentioned it for sure. I stacked the fire place and slung a match. Easy. They knew a bit about chimney craft when this joint was built. I made lemon tea and sprawled out on the floor.

Right...*Seize the Day*. That's how my bookworm phase kicked off. I spent the rest of that winter in much the same way. The library overlooked a small orchard. Half a dozen almond trees. When the blossoms appeared I daydreamed a lot. After they'd blown away I started reading in the garden. I took *Remembrance of Things Past* out to the fountain, which the chainsaw bloke had fixed up. He'd worked for nearly a week on odd jobs. It was the first really hot day of the year. The cicadas were tuning up.

I looked at the intro to *Remembrance*. The author, Proust, had been sick as a dog most of his life. He'd spent his last ten years in bed, scratching out these seven volumes on his knee. I looked at the text. I knew I'd picked another winner. I'd stretch this one. My summer was mapped out. The caretaker role I took seriously. Nothing was left undone. I kept things afloat easily. And looked at Proust every day, a few pages at a time. I still visited the statue now and then. Letters from Shelley I answered straight away. She sent photos of their kid, Mexico. We talked about music, and Lloyd's progress; Simon's name rarely came up. I'd mentioned his disappearance to Shelley, but that was all. I didn't know for sure who was looking at our mail. Probably no one. Not Wayne obviously. He would have kicked in the door before this if he'd suspected me of being other than bovine.

Simon's letters were brought by Mr Mordecai when he dropped in to check on the house. He'd ask me for an update. Simon never wrote to him. A bit nasty I thought. It could have been easily set up. It wasn't the risk. Simon just couldn't be bothered. Or maybe parents didn't fit into his Refugee script. Was I any better? Slightly. I wrote to Mum and Dad about once a month. It was hard to fill a small page. Adelaide seemed like a hundred years ago. It had only been two.

Late in March of 1970 I closed *Remembrance of Things Past*. I'd skip reading for a while. Proust had spoilt it for the others. There'd already been a cool day or two and the trees were beginning their ritual. Other changes hovered. Mr Mordecai had recently mentioned that his daughter Ruth would be returning from London soon. She planned to set up a law practice in Melbourne. Or join an existing firm. I forget which. Ruth didn't interest me. Simon had made her sound dreary. Which wasn't much to go on perhaps, but I had no reason to ask questions.

About the same time Shelley had been murmuring about coming home. Mexico was still a baby of course, and it was hard to make time for singing. Gigs were still out of the question. I don't know what Lloyd had imagined. A fortnight off and back to work perhaps. Anyway, he was understandably sick of spending his virtuosity on radio ads and had started rehearsals with a new band. He and Shelley weren't hostile, but it was awkward. In her next letter Shelley confirmed her arrival time in Melbourne. I mentioned this to Mr Mordecai. Yes. My friend could stay in Simon's room.

One night Ruth turned up unheralded. *She* wanted Simon's room. She'd heard of my presence from her father and had decided to frighten me off. Our meeting was a horror show. Second only to the Wayne affair. For a lawyer she was pretty straightforward. I was a gold digger. I was a parasite and a tyrant. I'd conned the scatterbrained Simon and also their poor old father. When was I leaving? A tough spot. I couldn't ask Mr Mordecai to back me against his own daughter. Simon couldn't be reached quickly, and would be powerless anyway. I stared at Ruth and didn't answer. She pushed past me. She actually had luggage. I couldn't believe it. I went and packed my rucksack. I'd accumulated nothing. I left my key and jumped through the window. I couldn't bitch, I'd had a good trot.

There was one complication. Shelley was due to arrive the next day. Right at that moment she'd be pointing out Hawaii to her starry-eyed babe. I'd promised to meet her at the airport. I could still do that. But there'd be no dreamy fireside. I had ninety-four dollars. I didn't want to crouch under a bridge. It was only autumn, but it was Melbourne. I got onto Punt Road and stuck my thumb out. I kept walking of course. I hadn't lost my reason. There'd be no Mark IV this murky night. At Johnston Street I turned towards Carlton. I'd been there maybe twice. After all this time my knowledge of the city was mainly from Simon's wall map. I'd hung it in the kitchen to study while the kettle boiled. I could have passed a cabby test by this time. If I'd been able to drive that is.

I was angry at Ruth for her split second timing. Shelley would laugh. She'd doubt my competence. What would she be like, anyway? We hadn't even spoken on the phone. She'd sung my songs though. My lyrics. She hadn't made a mess of them. Far from it. No point guessing anyway. We'd hit it off or we wouldn't. But where could I spend the night? What would Proust do? Sneeze probably. And the Norwegian author Hamsun? He'd tear up the ninety-four dollars.

It could have been much worse. There'd been no rain till dawn. I woke up and prised my kidneys from the ground. A plastic sheet next time. Not that I'd embarked on a career. I'd first attempted to sleep at about three o'clock,

I'd say. Before that I'd nursed hot drinks in a couple of all-nighters. There'd been no red carpet. I'd got the hint. Johnny's Green Room was the best. I'd milked nearly half an hour from that rude shelter. The owner left me alone but the snooker players needed a victim. I left. I figured sleeping out would be a step up. I wasn't so sure when I tested the earth in Argyle Square. At least there were bushes, and privacy.

When I stood up I realized I hadn't been completely alone. A figure spluttered in its sleep a few yards away. I could just make it out in the stingy light. A mass of curls sticking from a cardboard box, maybe a washing machine carton. Something like that. Here was a professional. The rain fell harder and even the seasoned trouper stirred. I hurried off. Conversation didn't appeal to me. I imagined how it might have gone:

"What brings you here, kiddo?"

"I've been cast out of my South Yarra home."

"Is that right? Whatever will you do?"

"Well, right now I'm off to the airport. A friend's arriving from California."

"Is that right?" Funny on the stage maybe. I didn't laugh. I looked for a bread shop. Far too early of course. Nothing was open. Well...Johnny's. They never closed. But I wasn't going back in there. Anyway, a bistro wasn't what I had in mind. My cash wouldn't last forever. I was in a mess. Shelley would be too. And her kid. My dumb luck had blundered off into the night. Could I manufacture more? I'd heard of people making their own luck. Nothing to do with rabbits' feet. It meant you didn't whimper, that's all. Well, I wasn't. And you didn't expect miracles. That was harder, given my track record.

The bustle rose in pitch. Trucks parked where they wanted, bread vans included. The drivers shooed me away. Wholesale only. Eventually blinds went up, radios crackled. An old guy with a Beatle haircut sold me three rolls and a banana. I scoffed them all at once. I popped the bag. I hadn't done that for years.

In the movies people had their names bawled out at airports. They took phone calls and memos. Maybe I could have tried something like that, but it didn't seem right. I had the arrival time. I'd show up and explain in person.

I got a bit lost looking for the airport road. I had to ambush people. I copped four shrugs and a life story. But information as well. At last I stood on the appropriate corner with my rucksack prominent. I'd heard many hitch hiker theories during my crash-pad days back in Adelaide. Some said you had to look sharp, write your destination on a big card. I wasn't equipped for this. Some had flags sewn onto their packs. Canada. Sweden. Others insisted you look as abject as possible. But I'd get the giggles if I tried that. One kid swore that starting to roll a cigarette was the key. Someone always pulled up to interrupt you. I didn't smoke, though.

A car stopped anyway after about ten minutes. A lady of thirty or so. Yes, she'd be passing near the airport. She had a scarf tied round her hair, pirate style. Her ears had copper peace signs dangling from them. The back seat was full of junk. She was moving to the country. She might pick fruit, she didn't know yet. Maybe she'd get into pottery. She knew a jeweller at some outpost. Maybe she'd look him up. Or maybe not. She was a qualified Free Spirit. Her head would be together any day now. Did I want to smoke something? No?

After what seemed like a week she dropped me at a turn-off. I set out for the airport buildings. The sky was cloudless. I'd got used to Melbourne weather, its chamelion mentality. I strapped on my rucksack and jogged. I was almost dry.

People stared at me in the airport lounge. They knew I'd slept out, I could tell. So much for my Sunday best, my loud overalls and black windcheater. But I had money, means of support. I couldn't be arrested. Just to make sure, I went to the toilet and stayed there. Public announcements came through but not clearly. I peeped out now and again to check the clock. At last I heard 'Arrival such and such now unloading' or whatever they say. No one looked at me now. The hustle was on. I swayed with the crowd and stood on my toes where possible. Passengers appeared in small groups. There might be customs. They'd have their job too of course. They might want to look down Shelley's shirt. They might want to change the baby. You couldn't assume.

No, no. Here she was. She had a soft hat and a striped ankle-length garment. The child Mexico clung to her back, peering out from a sling. Shelley was looking around anxiously. Not for me of course. She headed for the phones. I caught up.

"Shelley?"

"Wanda!"

Maybe she'd thought I'd be taller or something, I don't know. I felt weird anyway. It hadn't occurred to me until that moment how rough I must have looked, compared to the cheap but flattering photograph I'd sent. I owed her a story, and I'd keep it brief.

"Shelley, I'm on shaky ground. How can I put it… Do you know Ruth? Simon's sister?"

"Huh! Do I know Ruth!"

"She's back from London, and she kicked me out. As good as."

I gave Shelley the bulletin. She didn't panic or anything, but she seemed nervous. I had to explain without any hint of begging. A narrow plank.

"But Wanda, look at you! Where did you sleep?"

"Well, I didn't much. Ruth gave no warning. Now I'm prepared I'll be okay. I didn't want you to go there, or even phone. I didn't know how she'd react to you."

"Quite right, as it happens. It wouldn't have been pretty. Let me get you a coffee."

"Okay. Thanks. Shelley, have you got somewhere to…?"

"To stay? Yes. My mother lives here. Stake out the table, I'll order." She hurried to the counter, Mexico bouncing on her back.

"Cappuccino?" she called to me. I usually have black, but I nodded. I didn't want to bawl out. Shelley came back with a tray.

"Here you are, Wanda. This is my — ah, she's asleep."

Shelley plucked the kid from the sling, and held her on her lap. We chatted like polite strangers. Well, it was better than that, but it wasn't great. I had to be sure to camouflage my position. If I had to, I could shop around for a cardboard box like that tramp had. I'd do anything before stumbling into more cloudy economics. Shelley talked about Lloyd, and about my songs, our songs, which he was still using with his new band. Maybe there'd be royalties… Yeah, yeah. I only half listened. To me, the future meant that night's bed. Or its absence.

Mexico woke up and cried a bit. Shelley put her back in the pouch, and we left the coffee shop. She made a call and lined up her old room. I don't think her mother was very excited about it. Shelley chased up her bags. There were still a few cabs hanging around. Her mother lived on the esplanade at Middle Park. Would I like to be dropped somewhere?

In the city, I paid my share of the meter and hopped out. Shelley had given me her mother's number. We'd be in touch. I didn't quite know where I was. Ah! Yes I did. There was the railway station. Spencer Street. And here were the budget hotels. It was raining again. I decided to sidestep the camping out routine. I still had nearly ninety dollars. I went in to claim a room. No luck. Same story at the second joint. Full house again. Was there really a fight for these hovels? Hard to imagine. I'd been allowed to forget my colour. I'd been spoilt. I used the phone for the next one, and arranged things. I said I'd pay a week in advance. Fifteen dollars. They could still weasel out, of course, but it would be harder. I bought more bread rolls and stashed them in my bag. I stood watching the rain for a while. They needn't know I'd called from twenty yards away. I went in. There was no curtsey, but I got the key.

The room was a shocker. 'Like the movies,' I told myself. But it wasn't. For a start, it smelt. And a guy was coughing non-stop on the other side of the wall. *He* wasn't about to blow on a mournful cornet. I wondered if Simon was living as sordidly as this. He hadn't written for ages… I'd have to contact Mr Mordecai. Not straight away though. It would seem like telling tales on Ruth. But I'd call him soon. The Chocolate Girl was resting in peace, but maybe there'd be something I could do at the factory. Better than a cardboard sheet, that's what I had to remember.

I found the bathroom and showered. I changed into my

gardening clothes. Luckily, they'd just been washed. My damp overalls and stuff, I draped on a chair. I forced the window open and sat by it with a blanket round my shoulders. It was mid-afternoon, but felt like evening. Trams glowed, and some of the cars had their lights on. I thought of Argyle Square, where I'd spent the previous night. I started to get used to the room.

There was a bit of a runaround, but I got through at last. Simon's father sounded glum. Embarrassed even. Ruth hadn't been shy about announcing my departure. Mr Mordecai seemed relieved that I'd called. Almost like I'd been his own kid or something. It was the third day after Ruth's coup. Her father even suggested that I return to South Yarra. That Ruth and I could steer clear of each other, it was such a big house, and so on. He meant it, but he also knew I'd decline. He was appalled at the idea of my wanting factory work, but I suppose he could guess my options. He said I should apply in the standard way. Vacancies were frequent. I'd get in without his intervention.

The previous day, I'd spent ten dollars at a secondhand shop. Fresh overalls, jeans, two jumpers. All blue as it happened. No rips. After speaking to Mr Mordecai, I dressed up and got a tram to the factory. No delay. I started work that afternoon at four o'clock. The shift would rotate weekly. I had nearly fifty six dollars left. I felt like I'd got away with something.

The following Monday was my first day off. I was to meet Shelley outside the Art Gallery. We'd snoop around in there, and maybe stroll over to the Gardens if a gap appeared in the clouds. I felt a bit anxious. Our initial meeting had been poisoned by chance. We'd both been on wobbly skates. This time? Well, we'd soon know. Shelley had seemed okay on the phone.

When I left my room, the dingy hotel office was still closed. No greeting to be faked. I had plenty of time, and dawdled up Collins Street judging people. Well, not really judging. Guessing their stories. This pastime still amused me as much as ever. It was odd to think that a week before I'd been housebound. Only by habit, of course. Nothing had tied me down. I could easily have looked after the place, and still gone out exploring. South Yarra seemed so far away already. I'd sent my city address to Mum and Dad. They hadn't ever been to Melbourne. Spencer Street wouldn't mean a thing. And my new profession would please them. 'Packer' sounds more stable than 'Caretaker'. I'd never told them about the Chocolate Girl and her five hundred dollars. It would have thrown them into panic. Anyway, she was an industrial secret.

Near the Flinders Street Station I saw a bunch of people arrested, and flung into a van. Not hoods or anything. Vagrancy they could pin on you. Or drunk and disorderly. Stuff like that. The law baffles me sometimes. What's the point of nailing the derelict? Anyway, I didn't hang around. I had my own misdemeanour, my blackness. I thought I'd better watch out...

I'd arrived quite early, but I spotted Shelley in the distance in front of the Gallery. She was chucking Mexico up in the air. I started running, and got up close. She was focussed on the kid.

"Shelley!"

There was no hitch. We were soon talking and laugh ing about all kinds of stuff. We watched a council gang patching the road. We laughed some more. We threw bread at the doves. We skipped the exhibition. We felt too loud to frown at paintings. The sun was out, and we crossed to the Gardens. Mexico had a pram this time, Shelley's old one. It was English. She'd grown up in London.

We found a gate. It didn't matter what we saw, or missed. Lawns, ponds, ducks. It all looked okay. Mexico paddled in the fallen leaves. She could crawl a bit. She spotted a toadstool and headed straight for it. We had to stay on the ball. Shelley stuck her back in the pram, and gave her a bumpy ride. We stopped by a lake and checked the lilies. Shelley talked about moving from her mother's, and we agreed to find a place together.

"Will you rescue your stuff from Simon's garage?"

"My shapes?" That's what Shelley called her work.

"Yeah. You should hurry. Ruth might have bought a car already. She'll want that shed."

"You're right...although I don't particularly want to see her. We actually engaged in fisticuffs once, Ruth and I. A genuine confrontation, with punches. Like horrid little boys!"

"What was it about?"

"Oh, Simon and me. Our five minute affair. I think Ruth seeks drama. Certain people thrive on it, you know. As for my shapes..."

"Simon's father might have a key to the street door. You could load up without going into the house."

"A good idea. You say you get on well with him. Could you enquire for me?"

"Of course." I'd also have to speak to Mr Mordecai about collecting letters from Simon. I hadn't told Shelley of our correspondence. Simon had vanished, that's all she knew.

A rain shower worried the city for a while, then moved our way. Mexico woke up and we made a dash for the exit. The sun still shone on Domain Road, and we drifted along it. We bought a paper to look for a house. No luck. Monday's a dud for that stuff. Shelley phoned a rental office, and set something up for the following morning. She would dress up in her toff clobber to deal with the agent. I'd lurk somewhere out of sight, and trust her decision on the house. A foolproof strategy. Serious rain came in at about four. By then we were almost back at the Gallery. The scenic route. We arranged to meet the next day, after Shelley had looked at places. It was starting to get a bit cold for the kid. We stopped a cab. The driver loaded up the pram. Shelley hopped in, and I handed her the baby. The door shut with her Afghan coat sticking out. They drove off, and I ran for shelter. Only a few yards.

It was one of those orange-lit shops with a jukebox on every table. I ordered toasted cheese. I'd be paid soon. Maybe Shelley had found something already. She was a bit later than I'd expected. I got a cherry coke. I found Janis Joplin on the machine, and dropped a coin in. Shelley turned up. She looked triumphant. She waved down my impatience and ordered coffee.

"Well then, Wanda. I told him I'd ring within the hour. I nearly took it on the spot. He showed me others, but —" She whipped out her notebook and sketched the floor plan. It didn't matter to me. I was living in Spencer Street. I'd move anywhere. Anywhere that had a roof. But I didn't interrupt her flourishes. There were three or four rooms and a courtyard. It wasn't far from town. No, of course it didn't smell. Only of wet paint. It would be available in three weeks. It was in Fitzroy. Naturally, I agreed, and Shelley made the call. Nothing to it.

***

A truck took Shelley's statues to the new joint. She'd conned the agent into letting her use the courtyard straight away. The chisels and things she packed up and kept herself. It felt a bit strange at South Yarra. I didn't go near the house. There'd been no hitch getting the key to the garage. Mr Mordecai would arrange for letters from Simon to appear in my locker at work. Plain wrap. We were still looking over our shoulders. Crazy probably, after so long.

A couple of days before I was due to move, I finally got some news. Simon had strayed from his nest in The Rocks, his hide-out.

Robbers' Creek
22nd May 1970

Dear W,

I'm becoming slack again, I know. Sorry if I caused anxiety. I'm head down on a new venture. Two years of seediness and caution is enough. It was driving me nuts. For several weeks, I'd been strolling out a little, usually around Circular Quay. On one such promenade, I met a vigorous and sincere gent by the name of Bartos. He manufactures and distributes a herbal tonic known as Eternia, whose contents are, of course, secret. It smells vaguely of aniseed, but the active ingredient is apparently odourless. He has to import it from Greece, his birthplace. His grandmother discovered the properties of this vital plant many years ago. Attempts to grow it in Australia have failed repeatedly. Bartos has saved a number of lives, yet he exists humbly amid sneers and ridicule. No one believes he's in his mid-fifties. He looks and speaks as though he were my age. (Which, incidentally, he guessed at once, despite my 'greyness'.)

Here at Robbers' Creek, we live very simply in a shack built by my host's own hands. Apart from basic furniture, there is a brewing contraption housed in a small shed. Unfortunately, Bartos has a cash flow problem. (You should see his ancient truck.) Very soon now, he'll run out of the herb on which everything hinges.

As you know, my income and my lifestyle don't quite match. I'd amassed $8000 by the time I met Bartos. It is now in his keeping. Without giving details, I told him that my money had come from confectionery, a destructive commodity in his view. He shook his head, but accepted my tainted currency for the cause. However, it's not really enough. It would be far more efficient if he could bring back a respectable shipload of the priceless balm. He's sailing for Europe in just over a month.

This leads me to the point — please advertise the piano. A Bosendorfer in such condition should bring close to $30,000. Start higher. Send the cash to my old room at The Rocks. I'm ahead on rent, and I've asked the landlord there to expect a package and hold it for me.

I've been using the product myself for seventeen days. I think my memory is growing sharper. Also my vision. Bartos knew a chap whose sight was apparently weaker than mine before he discovered Eternia. Now he's amateur squash champion of Western Victoria. Please don't tell Father. He'd call it snake oil.

Counting on you,
S.

A mug, or what? I couldn't believe it. Simon had the knack alright. He was a born victim, despite his millions, or potential millions. And who was I? Head Nurse? What could I do? The piano, of course, would stay in its corner. I could write and explain my new situation — He'd have to ask Ruth, et cetera. But what else? I couldn't laugh in Simon's face, and besides, this Bartos had already grabbed the savings. If I told Mr Mordecai, he might cut his son off completely. If I didn't, money would keep flowing to Sydney. Four hundred for Bartos, two hundred for Simon, or whatever it was. Though not for long, admittedly, with Mr Bartos abroad.

I'd have to confide in Shelley. She'd refer to the dilemma as a 'pickle', but she might have answers. I stuck the letter back in my locker. I'd arrived at work early, so I'd have time for coffee. Too late now. The siren had gone off. Bliss Bars don't wait.

At about nine thirty the next morning I phoned Shelley. Her mother sounded put out, but called her to the phone. I gave no hints at the topic, but told her we had to talk. No, not about the house. We'd move in the following day, as planned. Yes, it was something urgent. Not life and death, but urgent. The same coffee shop, the one with the jukebox? Why not. We'd been back to it a couple of times since house-hunting day.

I was there in fifteen minutes, and didn't have to wait long. Shelley came in flustered. She'd fought with her mother about leaving Mexico behind. But she'd swung it.

"I must be back there in two hours. What's happening?"

"Simon's made a dumb move."

"Oh really? And the prime minister had a shave this morning."

"No, listen... *Really* dumb... He and I have been writing. Have a look at this."

I fished out Simon's letter, and Shelley scanned it. She was trying to look serious. Fat chance. We both burst out. The other customers stared.

"Any ideas? Simon's on the run, don't forget." I was whispering. This set Shelley off again. She lost it completely this time. The funny side was dominant. I couldn't deny that. I got caught up again myself. It was useless. We had to leave. Mirth alarms people. We ran as fast as we could. We sobered up, more or less. It was pretty fragile though. We stood outside a trinket shop in Lonsdale Street. There were Greeks everywhere. It wouldn't have taken much to start us up again. We moved on quietly, before they got the wrong end of the stick. We crossed the road and stood near the hospital gate. We forced ourselves. We dared each other. We were determined. We became rational, and we talked...

Bartos would be extinct in a month. He'd be roasting a sheep in dusty Athens. Or not. He might choose to wolf cakes at Kirribilli. It didn't make any difference. He'd be gone, with Simon's loot burning his Levis. No use dragging the cops in. They might catch Bartos, but our Fugitive would pay up as well. It was double or nothing. Shelley couldn't just take off for Sydney. I couldn't either. What for, anyway? This operator might be armed, or anything. And Simon probably wouldn't co-operate. He was mesmerized. He had a new obsession. He'd be rock solid. He had a guru. It wasn't easy. There was no point fantasizing. We'd need an accomplice. Simon's father?

"Shelley, he'll be furious. What can he do, anyway? He's not a gangster."

"He may know someone. For a start, he could hire a detective."

"A private eye? You're as crazy as Simon."

"Not at all. Such people are useful. A detective could survey Simon's city room. Bartos will almost certainly accompany him to collect his additional treasure. Why wouldn't he? This man's probably met a thousand bunglers. He'll have recognized our friend as a perfect specimen. He'll be careless. Nonchalant — "

"But what then? Our bloke'll report to us, that's all, and we're no better off."

"He can get a photo, if he's any good."

"A photo? What use is that? Bartos will have a beard down to his waist, I guarantee it. Maybe even a real one, but its days are numbered."

"Yes, yes, I realize he'll be in costume, but... You'll really think *I'm* crazy this time... I have an intuition. A suspicion, if you like."

"What do you mean?"

"Did Simon ever discuss his student days with you?"

"There was something about a 'school for boys'. It sounded like a prison — "

"Hm? Oh, you heard that story? But no, I meant university. Did he tell you about his court appearance?"

"No, nothing like that. I only knew him for a couple of weeks, remember."

"Well, there was a kind of scandal — No, no, not Simon's scandal. He was just unfortunate... There was a chap there, an older student, who organized entertainment, some of it authorized, some not. Anyhow, one night — I think it was an end of term do, he promoted a little performance in a tent. Pornographic, by any definition. The writhing silhouette was blatant, and someone filed a complaint. I can't recall the details, but Simon had been close by, distributing pacifist leaflets, or some such thing. Why his testimony was so important, I've no idea, but he was summoned as a witness, and this other chap wound up paying a large fine. I think he even did some time — "

"And swore to get even with Simon. And you think it's Bartos. That's one in a million, Shelley. And Simon would know him, anyway."

"Not necessarily. The fellow had been an outstanding drama student before this incident. I saw him in a couple of productions. He was extraordinary. He could portray anyone he liked — not that he'd have to be a genius for this little stunt with Simon. I'm sorry, I didn't mean that... It bears this chap's arrogant stamp, Wanda. Especially the name."

"Bartos? What do you mean?"

"The student was called Barton. Barton McQueenie. Nothing on its own, of course, any more than the rest. But it's possible don't you agree?"

"Hm!"

"I'd know McQueenie from a photograph, bearded or not."

"Shelley, if it's the same guy, he'd be onto Simon's situation. He'd just blackmail him, or something like that."

"Barton McQueenie miss a chance to perform? Not likely. Anyhow it's only a theory. We need a picture."

"Therefore we need a gumshoe. Therefore I'm to speak to Simon's father, right? Very exciting, but I can't believe in it for a second."

"Let's do it, Wanda. Phone him."

I could never have imagined it. Mr Mordecai had a fit. He was speechless at first. I had to keep calling into the phone. His self-assurance had dried up. Then he made me tell him again. I even read out some of the letter. I think he cried, I'm not sure. Simon had found a new level of incompetence. It was unbelievable... I brought up the detective idea, but not Shelley's hunch, or whatever it was, about McQueenie. Mr Mordecai was completely stunned. But he agreed to contact an agency.

"Now it's detectives," he kept murmuring. I tried to calm him down. I don't know what I said. Eventually, some of his dignity returned. A meeting was arranged for the following evening. At Fitzroy, our new address. The first available sleuth, and Mr Mordecai, and us. A house-warming party. We'd need pretzels. Maybe something to drink...

Shelley moved the next morning. She had a mountain of stuff. It had filled the spare room at Middle Park for three years. Her mother was 'glad to see the back of it'. Now that she had a spare room again, she was more relaxed. She'd given Shelley a lemon cake. I'd just started the day shift again. By five thirty, I was hopping off the tram in Brunswick Street. I had an old airways bag now, as well as my rucksack. Too many clothes. A failed hobo.

I'd only seen the courtyard of the new joint, so far. And peered in the windows. It was cheap. That was the main thing. My share would be less than I'd been peeling off at the fleapit. Shelley had both the keys. She let me in. There was junk in the corridor. Twenty or thirty empty boxes. Tea-chests, cartons, all sorts. Ones you could sleep in at a pinch. I dropped my bags in the vacant room. The arrangement was obvious — Shelley's bedroom had a cubicle for the kid. Mexico was in there already, asleep in a cot. Shelley's old cot. The kitchen was set up too. A table and six chairs — the hangaround area. There was no living room, or anything like that.

Our meeting was scheduled for seven thirty. I'd worked till midnight, before switching to the day shift. I wanted to flop down for an hour. The bed question arose. I felt like a clown. Furniture hadn't crossed my mind. Shelley had extra stuff, a roll-up mattress and a sleeping bag. Gratefully accepted. I'd have to go shopping again — more objects, more clutter. Hmm. Shelley would sing out at seven. I curled up.

A jug and four glasses sat on the table. We had lemon cordial but it looked like water. We felt like big shots. United Nations or something. Mr Mordecai stared at the lino. He'd been kinghit by this fiasco. Our private eye was a bit late. Only a few minutes. The brass knocker banged, and Shelley jumped up. *Here* he was, all smiles. No tie, no hat, nothing. About thirty. It was a big job for him, an interstate trip. He'd been made a generous offer. Usually, people came to *his* place, his office — I figured he'd have *that* wrong too. Fluoro lit, probably, and spotless. He didn't inspire confidence. Introductions happened. Alan Gilbert he was called. He sat down.

"Mind if I smoke?" He was still smiling.

"It's the *least* you can do!" I blurted out.

He gave me an odd look. So did Shelley. Mr Mordecai hadn't heard. I got an ashtray, and Gilbert fumbled in his raincoat. He did have a raincoat. Out came the cigarettes. Filters! I should have guessed.

But I soon had a different angle. This Gilbert was thorough. He listened to our weaving chatter, and scribbled hieroglyphs on a pad. He studied Simon's photo. We clued him up on the fake greyness. He asked every possible relevant question, plus a few obscure ones. He said he'd have Bartos on film in two days, wherever he was. Gilbert had contacts, he had the best camera known to Man. We'd have our portrait.

Good. Shelley's theory, of course, hadn't been aired. All hung on the snapshot. If it did turn out to be McQueenie... Well, we'd see how Gilbert handled the first bit. There might be something more challenging for him...

Mr Mordecai hadn't taken part. He'd hardly even looked up. How much he'd understood was anyone's guess. It was left to Shelley and me to deal with Gilbert. The detective and Mr Mordecai left together just before ten. The kid hadn't squeaked. Shelley dug out the lemon cake she'd got from her mother. We'd forgotten all about it. Shelley had a brandy. I had the wit to decline. Six thirty I'd have to wake up. Changing to a different shift is tricky. You need a day or so to retune.

Our new house felt okay. We'd drag logs home. We'd try out the ancient stove. It would be a laugh... Not tonight though.

Gilbert didn't muck around. Three days it took him. He phoned Monday morning. I had the day off. He'd snapped a couple of rolls. He sounded proud. Professional though. Not like a Mouth or anything. He'd visit us. We were favoured customers. Shelley was giving Mexico a bath. I gave her the news, and went into the yard to gaze at the statue. Shelley came out towelling the kid's hair.

"Cross your fingers, Wanda."

"You *hope* it's McQueenie, don't you?"

"Well, at least we'd have a chance. What did Gilbert say?"

"Nothing. He's got the shots, and he's close by."

"Did you think he'd be any good?"

"Gilbert? No. Well, not at first. I thought he – Shelley! The door!"

We tripped over each other. I got there first.

"Mr Gilbert! Show us!"

"Okay, okay." He had a briefcase this time. I made him sprint down the passage. Shelley cleared a spot on the kitchen table. Gilbert laid out his wares.

"Yes! It's him!" Shelley had picked up one of the enlargements. Then she wasn't sure. She handed me the kid. She grabbed another blow-up. I'd got one thing right. Bartos had a beard. It was a hell of a thing. Like Ned Kelly. You wouldn't even ask him for a light. Could this be the great McQueenie? Was this dramatic art at its purest? A caricature? A conman in dress uniform? Impossible.

"Yes. It's him." Shelley tossed down the pictures. "It's him. I'm certain."

"What are you people doing to me? If you knew the answer, why was I brought in?"

"It was only a guess, Mr Gilbert. We needed the photo. Please sit down. Would you excuse us for a moment?"

"It's your money."

Shelley dragged me up the passage to my room. I was still holding the kid.

"Wanda! Should we let him in on it? Should we tell him what we know about McQueenie?"

"Wait a minute! The guy in the photo's a ham. You said McQueenie – "

"There's no doubt! It's definitely Barton McQueenie. He knows his target. He knows Simon lives in storyland. He knows our friend can't resist a stereotype."

I was a bit like that myself, with my Hollywood detectives, and my hobo fantasies. I didn't own up though.

"Yeah, you're right, Shelley. I guess Simon does dream a bit. Okay! So let's say it's McQueenie. What more can Gilbert do?"

"I don't know yet. We'll lay our cards down, and see what he suggests. There's nothing to lose. All this is confidential... Besides, he already knows we can't go to the police, and why."

"Shouldn't we ask Mr Mordecai? He's paying."

"He's placed us at the wheel. You saw his condition the other night."

The detective was smoking in the courtyard, admiring the sculpture. Shelley hustled him back to the kitchen. She gave him the yarn. Every detail. The porno show, Simon's unlucky proximity to it, Barton McQueenie's conviction... And now his disguised reappearance.

"Any ideas, Mr Gilbert?"

He shuffled his feet. His mouth hung open. He blinked a few times. It didn't look promising. You can't always tell though.

"McQueenie's an actor, you say?"

"I know it sounds funny, Mr Gilbert." Even Shelley was embarrassed.

"No. No. I'm just thinking…"

"Can you do anything?"

He didn't answer. There were no clues at first. Then we got a twitching jaw, and steely competence appeared in his eyes… It started to look encouraging. Yes! He'd accept the commission.

* * *

Shelley's career had been on hold for well over a year. She hardly even sang at home. Sometimes with the radio, that was all. Her contact with Lloyd was pretty steady. He was touring with his new band. Things had come together quickly — they'd played in Los Angeles several times, and done smaller gigs in the Northwest, and a few in Canada. They'd already cut a record, a single. My lyrics had been used on one side. Lloyd hadn't asked me. That would have been Unhip I guess. I didn't care anyway. I was flattered, if anything. Since starting at the factory, I hadn't had so much time for coming up with new stuff. I had a couple of things in the works, not quite ready yet. 'Nameless Dread' was one of them. And 'Madeleine Cake'. No music of course. Lloyd's old demo tapes had scared me off from that side of the business. After hearing his fancy arrangements, I couldn't be satisfied with three chords any more. Besides, there was no guitar in the house.

Shelley had been mumbling for a while about singing. She'd spoken of forming a band, or maybe a duo. She'd known lots of Melbourne players in the old days. It wouldn't be hard to chase them up. Some would have work already, of course. Others would still be fine-tuning their craft in lounge rooms, ankle deep in beercans, their heads full of angels…

About the middle of June, we decided we should have a night out, before we got too old. A few beers, live music. A pretty loose game plan. Mexico could sprawl out at Middle Park, marvel at Granny's T.V., stay overnight…

It was a Friday. I was to meet Shelley at six. I forget the name of the pub. She hadn't wanted to wait for me at home. I turned up a bit early. Shelley was near the bar, talking to a couple of blokes. Hippies you'd have to say. City ones. They hadn't transcended alcohol. I was soon spotted.

"Darling!" Shelley hadn't called me that before. She was waving her arms around. I got through the crush.

"Wanda! Meet…Zippo and Zigzag!"

"I'm Ziggy," one explained, "and this is my friend, Pip."

"Hi. I'm Wanda."

Ziggy had a knitted cap and a cross in his ear. He grinned all the time. His overcoat was ex-army, with a peace-sign on the lapel. A bit of a plait hung over his collar. The other guy, Pip, had a corduroy jacket and flannel shirt. And straight shoulderlength hair parted in the middle. He smoked little brown cigarettes from India. Beedies they were called. Pip was the Serious One. They'd all gone on talking straight away. I'd have to catch up. I signalled the barman, and got a pint.

Shelley had steered the chatter round to reincarnation. Suddenly she was an expert. Pip and Ziggy knew even less, and she got away with it. All three were Old Souls. They agreed on this at once. They rattled off famous names from history. Yeah, they'd all been round before. No room for doubt. They lifted their drinks and drained them. Pip chased through his coat and found a rumpled cheque. He was known here, he'd cash it, we'd have scotch. Ziggy grinned at me.

"C'mon Wanda, do your bit."

He wanted me to gulp the rest of my pint. Good idea. I might recall a crucial detail from the eighth century. You never know. I did it in two hits. The scotch appeared. Pip was angry.

"That bourgeois prick. He sees me three times a week, and now he wants to make a hassle."

"You cashed it though?" A desperate Ziggy.

"Course. How'd I get *this?* Cheers!"

Pip distributed the shots, and we put them away. I was starting to warm up. Ziggy produced tobacco, and a small machine. He made a cigarette pop out.

"Darling! How wonderful! Could you roll me one?"

A sure sign. Shelley was blotto. And so early. The T.V. News was still on. I tried not to think too far ahead…

A band thumped. I could feel it through the table, but I couldn't lift my head. It went on and on. I'd look up soon. Any minute now… A choppy guitar dominated for a while. It cut right through. People were jumping everywhere. Someone shook my arm for ages, and went away again. The music stayed… Its volume suddenly fell slightly, and a roar went up. I found strength somewhere, and squeezed a hand under my chin. A short guy was creeping onto the stage. He was laughing and waving, and shuffling very slowly. He had an old suit over a T-shirt. I think he was a Maori. He shook his hair around, and the crowd yelled even louder. Then he did it. He sang the best stuff I'd ever heard. There was spilt beer spreading on the table, but I couldn't move again. No chance. I cried straight into the puddle. The bloke on stage had about five octaves. And tremolo. I watched through my tears. I had to keep breathing. I remembered that much. It was a privilege to be at ringside. That hadn't escaped me either. But otherwise there was nothing. No past, nothing. I was an Audience. Full time.

"That's how it's done! That's how it's done! That's how it's done!" Over and over I heard this. Maybe a dozen times. It was Shelley, bawling in my ear. She was sitting right next to me. She may have been there for hours, I didn't know. She varied her chant. "That's what singing is! That's what singing is!" I didn't need persuading. The song ended. The crowd kept yelling and stamping on the floor. Those two guys came over. What were they? Flip and Flop or something. It didn't matter much. We all remembered each other okay. The grinning one spoke.

"Shall we go?"

Was he crazy, or tone deaf, or what? I shook my head and pointed at the stage. They all laughed. Where had I been? That was the encore! Stuff like that. I started to get angry. They couldn't trick *me*. Then the lights went on. It was the end alright. People were picking up velvet bags and things. Bouncers were milling around. We went with the flow. There was no option this time. In the street, I woke up a bit. But I didn't have a clue what was happening. I didn't know this new pub. I didn't even know the suburb.

"Why don't you come round for coffee? Pip's got something to smoke. It's not far."

Ah! Pip and Ziggy, that's right. I remembered now.

"Why not?" Shelley said. I didn't bother to argue. We linked arms and kind of marched. No one tried to sing. It would have been Uncool, after hearing that guy back there...

Ziggy and Pip's house was squalid. Just like the Adelaide joints I'd known in the old days. Different posters of course — Woodstock had been and gone. But otherwise the same. They tossed the newspapers and things off the couch and chairs. They were sorry their stereo was busted. Shelley and Ziggy flopped down on the sofa and horsed around. Pip went out into the yard to find his stash. I stretched out on the floor, among the scattered papers.

Saturday. It was late. I knew that without checking. I'd missed work. Pip snored next to me. We were lying on a single mattress. I remembered the singing. That Maori guy's voice.

***

By Tuesday, I was starting to think straight. I'd worked Monday, my scheduled day off, to force myself back on track. The detective had phoned Sunday night, with a thumbs up. I'd lost faith in him, I must admit. But somehow, he'd recovered the cash. Would we ever know the details? Probably not. Gilbert wasn't obliged to tell us a thing. He'd speak to Mr Mordecai about his fee. Tuesday afternoon, I went to my locker. Simon had written from his city quarters.

Wanda,

The most terrible thing has happened. Bartos has been swindled! It was all so fast. I don't know how it came about. I've gone over and over it in my head. Everything's lost. Here's what I remember. We were having a quiet drink last night. I stuck to soda water. Bartos, just for once, drank spirits, but he certainly wasn't drunk. There were two men nearby who *were* drunk. Or seemed to be. I keep going over it. They'd been talking quite loudly about a film they were producing. An 'adults only' sort of film, you know what I mean. They were so loud, they *had* to be drunk, but now I don't know. Apparently, one of their backers had reneged. Also their male lead, a Scottish guy, who'd been exactly right, et cetera. They seemed really upset. They were drunk, I'm sure. One of them finally staggered out leaving the other one to mope on his own. Poor Bartos took pity on the man, I suppose. He went over and talked quietly with him. The man seemed to calm down. Bartos *is* a comfort, there's no doubt of that. I didn't want to interfere with his works, and I remained at the bar.

After nearly an hour, Bartos came over to me and said he was taking the man somewhere, and that he'd be back later on. He apologized for having to desert me. He said he'd return as soon as possible. What could I say? I know the kind of man he is. Anyway, he came back quite soon, saying he *had* been able to help, and so forth. He slept on my couch last night, and this morning went out early to meet with his new friend.

Wanda! What can I do? Bartos came back almost in tears. He'd offered to bail out this man with his own money! He'd handed over the $8000 I'd given him, and his savings as well, probably not much, but everything he had. And now this stranger has vanished overnight! He didn't even *look* like a film-maker! But how could I have foreseen such recklessness from my Bartos? Poor trusting Bartos. He's due to sail in a few days. With no capital for his herbs!!

Sell the piano, Wanda! Accept $25,000. Sell it, *please*. At once!!! It's all so terrible.

S.

Entertaining news. But I couldn't let the cat out yet. Simon would have to wring his hands for a bit longer. Until Bartos ambled away, back into the wings. Otherwise, anything could happen. Simon was easy prey, of course, but he wasn't a coward. He'd be capable of pulling the alleged Greek's beard, and lecturing him on ethics. Any amount of tomfoolery. I'd have to play dumb for now. I wondered how much McQueenie had lost, on top of the eight thousand. It could be five hundred or five thousand. Anyone's guess. Whatever it was, the private eye had it in his sock. Fair enough too. A one-off scam in the line of duty.

When I reached home, I noticed Mr Mordecai's car parked nearby. He and Shelley were chatting at the kitchen table. He'd brought flowers and fancy cakes. He was in better condition, of course, and grateful for our help, and so on, but he didn't seem elated. Okay, apart from Gilbert's fee, the eight thousand dollars was back in the family. But I guess 'My son the dupe' persisted in the abstract...

"Ah! Wanda! Thank you, thank you. There's cheese strudel. Also cherry... How can we cure young Simon? Why does he do this to me? I know. I know he's in hiding, his opportunities are limited. But who created the situation? Not you or I. The boy walks into these things... Do you know what he studied at the university? Mathematics! Not Economics. Not Business Admin. Mathematics! He liked its purity! That's what he said. Ha! Purity! Circles in the dust! And for what? Where's it got him, Wanda?"

Even Mr Mordecai hadn't gauged the full depth of Simon's idiocy. He didn't know of his renewed wish to sell the piano. That data was still in my pocket. I wasn't about to flash it. The idea of the Bosendorfer thundering into the pit with everything else would have finished him off for sure.

"Simon's an idealist, Mr Mordecai." A flimsy response, I realize that.

"Idealist! He's a dreamer! He thinks everyone's a paragon of some kind. If you dispute this, then you're a cynic. That's his attitude. What am I supposed to do?"

What was *I* supposed to do? Pretend to argue with Mr Mordecai when in fact I agreed? Or shaft Simon, my benefactor? It was sticky ground. I said nothing... Shelley poured out more coffee. Mexico woke up, and she went off to the rescue. I tried out the cherry strudel. A bit of rain heckled the kitchen window. I switched on the electric heater. The stove had turned out to be a dud.

"How's the factory, Wanda? You're sick to the teeth?"

"Well, it's no mental stretch, but I'm glad of the job... There's nothing else, is there? Maybe in the office?"

"As far as I'm aware, no. People hold onto such work."

I wondered if Mr Mordecai ever thought about the Chocolate Girl. It had been so long ago. Anyway, I was glad he never mentioned her. Even at this point, I'd have made the same decision. A low profile was still my priority.

"What will become of my son?" How could I reassure the man? I could easily imagine Simon getting mugged as he distributed soup in West Melbourne. Or visiting strangers in prison, and finding himself cast as the fall guy. Neither of which bore the glow of triumph.

"He'll find his way, Mr Mordecai." Daggy, I know, but I was cornered.

"Ha!"

I stared at the patch of grey sky. Our low rent glimpse of the firmament. Nothing was said. After about ten minutes, Mr Mordecai sighed and stood up.

"I must be off, Wanda. See Miss Dale at Personnel. She can take your name at least. You're inside our gate already. That counts for something. It's up to you."

We'd reached the front door. Shelley had come out with the kid. We thanked Mr Mordecai for the flowers and things… Not at all, it was nothing, we'd dealt with the detective. He strolled to his car, head down. We closed the door and went back to the kitchen. I showed Shelley the letter. We chuckled a bit, but it was nothing like last time, when Simon had first drawn our attention to Bartos.

Two days later, I was back on the midnight shift, the allnighter. These changeovers were tampering with my sanity. I didn't know how much longer I could last. For nearly two months I'd been juggling with my sleep. The previous day, I'd applied to Miss Dale for something in the office. Nothing at present. She'd written down my name. On Friday night I found a note from Simon. He said that Bartos had shuffled away, crestfallen, vowing never to return. Simon hoped his friend hadn't done anything desperate.

On Saturday, I scribbled out my exposé of McQueenie, told Simon how we'd hired Gilbert, and so on. I suggested that he try to be more careful in future. Something like that. I still didn't bother to mention Ruth, or my departure from South Yarra. I posted the letter on my way to the Saturday night shift. Sunday afternoon, I slept. And Sunday night.

Monday was my day off. I woke before dawn, feeling lively. I put on my windcheater and two jumpers, and left the house. Daylight was an hour away. I took backstreets. Unexplored ones where possible. I was headed for town, via Carlton. There weren't many people around. A few early starters, factory workers. Some looked desperate, others had passed that stage. They all stooped. No one ran. There weren't too many dawn joggers back then. Some houses had lights on, and radios. I couldn't imagine starting my day in the company of a pumped-up DJ. Maybe it's different if you've already abandoned your life.

I'd woken up excited about my day off, but already it seemed to be circling down the drain. Despair was creeping up. I pinned my hopes on sunrise. And Lygon Street. I'd find some kind of action there, something to look at. Even on the night I'd slept out, Carlton at this time of the morning had cheered me up.

Not today though. Lygon Street was sluggish. People looked sad and weary. Even the Italians, who normally got it right. There was a grey blanket over the world. It was no good to me. I didn't wade in it. I thought the city might be an improvement...

I started to think about Shelley, and her neglected singing. That Maori vocalist had certainly knocked her out, the night of our drinking binge. His performance should have livened her up. But nothing had changed. It was now over a week since that show. Maybe she'd forgotten what his music had generated. I hadn't forgotten. Shelley read magazines, and did crosswords. Lloyd sent her money. She was getting lazy. How could people slide so fast? Maybe *I* was sliding too. I was twenty one already. And what had I done? A spot of futile gardening. I'd read a few books. Dragged Simon from the current a couple of times... Boxed at least four million chocolate bars... And written songs — this was the only bit that amounted to anything. This I'd have to keep doing, if I didn't want to break long service records at the factory.

Ralph Messer, my day-shift boss in the packing room, had been working there since 1948. He wasn't even ashamed. *He* was the one who'd mentioned it. And he wasn't a complete dunce, either. He knew a couple of foreign languages, and had been a school teacher for a while. The kids had been too cruel, or something. I could see you had to be careful, or you might easily wake up doomed. There'd be holes in your slippers. People would bring you puddings. It would all be over, while you tossed up between Law and Medicine.

"NOT ME!" I shouted. Quite loud, like a fanatic. Luckily, no one turned or came up to advise me. I passed opposite Argyle Square, where I'd had to sleep out a while back. I wondered if that guy still hung around there. I wondered if tramps pegged out territory, and if so, whether bigger tramps respected their wishes. I thought again about the cardboard box method of shelter. I tried to calculate the maximum level of dignity that a vagrant could hope to maintain. All kinds of theoretical gibberish clawed its way into my head. I wasn't in good nick.

Police Headquarters loomed ahead, but I didn't bother about taking a detour. Indifference it was, not audacity, or anything like that. I saw the old courthouse over the road. I'd heard that Ned Kelly had been strung up somewhere in that building. I started running, sprinting... I'd get coffee somewhere. I could tell already that the sun wouldn't show up on time. Maybe later. At morning tea.

The caffeine worked a bit. I'd had two strong ones. I plodded on. I'd catch a suburban train. That was my new scheme. I'd get off at a random spot. I wouldn't even look at the sign. I'd be someone else for a couple of hours. Like seeing a movie. Just for a couple of hours.

At Flinders Street, people were mostly coming *into* the city. I picked a terminus, and got a ticket. But I wouldn't go to the end of the line. I'd hop out and ramble. Four or five miles from town would do. Then I could walk back if I wanted. I found the right platform. The train turned up. There was hardly anyone travelling in *this* direction. Schoolkids in uniform. An old bloke with no teeth... After three or four stops, they'd all jumped ship.

I strolled up and down the carriage calling out "TICK-ETS!" I ignored a couple more stations, then I stood near the door. I was in a weird state. The train slowed down. I saw something blue sticking out from under a newspaper. It was a woollen cap, a CATS beanie. I jammed it on. It would help me to be someone else. I got out.

The suburb was dreary. That didn't matter. It was a frontier. You could tell where the sun was supposed to be. I was east of the city. I shambled up and down the main road. I took sidestreets if I happened to like their names... But I felt old. Old and finished. That's what I kept thinking. I was in zombie territory.

I entered a secondhand shop. That can be a good move if you want surprises. There were broken toys, clothes, furniture they'd never unload, kitchen stuff, records. The usual. The bloke watched me closely. As if I'd dash into the street clutching *this* crap. He couldn't stop watching. He got up and stood near the door. He tried to be casual about it. He pretended to move a couple of lousy chairs. I started trying on coats. They weren't swish. But I'd never even put on a coat, except as a kid. It felt pretty good, I had to admit. I called the morbid owner across.

"How much for this?"

He held up three fingers.

"Okay. I'll wear it now." I gave him twenty dollars, and he went over to the till. He kept looking at me in a blotchy mirror.

"I got a good bike," he growled.

"Show me." I had nothing else to do. It looked alright for twelve bucks. I hadn't ridden a bike for years either.

"Okay." I wheeled it out. I did up my coat, and wobbled into the traffic. The bike was a rattler, but the breeze blew on me. That was the main thing. If a street sloped, I took it. Direction didn't matter, it was my day off. I tried to make up tunes. No luck. Lloyd's department. Or others of his kind... But I'd grow rich anyway. Maybe not rich, but I wouldn't be Ralph Messer. I wouldn't be in the packing room for twenty years. I'd eat scorpions first. I'd hollow out a tree, and slumber within. Should my presence be required in distant parts, I'd snare a touchy steed and gain dominion over its mind.

Wasn't a bad day off really…

* * *

Our lease at Fitzroy was about to expire. We'd signed for six months. At least, Shelley had. Officially, I didn't exist. That suited the agent, and it suited me. It was early November. We'd have to decide soon. Staying would be no problem. Shelley just had to provide another signature. But things weren't quite the same.

I was still in the packing room. In fact, I'd already set a new standard of persistence. No one else had been able to deal with the shift changes for more than three months. I'd doubled that. For Ralph Messer, the twenty-years-plus man, it was different. He always stayed on the 8-4. Apparently, supervisors on the other two shifts would last eighteen months, on average. Messer had these stats at his fingertips. He wasn't shy about passing them on. I guess it underlined his own stamina, or something. Now that I'd easily out-distanced all the other packers, Messer saw me as a potential heir to *his* position. He'd be retiring in three years. He'd started harping on this detail. In the context of his mammoth career, three years was nothing. An eight bar coda, a party trick. But not for me. I tried to put him straight.

"I won't be here in three years, Ralph."

"Of course you will. You're cut out for it. You're not one of these fly-by-nights. You have a future. It won't be *my* decision of course, but it stands to reason. Show loyalty, and you'll be promoted. *I* was lucky. I knew old A. S. Mordecai from my army days. He took a chance. He slotted me straight in as a supervisor. Mind you, if I hadn't cut the mustard, I'd have been shown the door. My record at the Education Department hadn't been impressive, I can tell you. But A. S. took a chance, and I didn't let him down. Nor have I let his son down. I don't know what the next generation will bring. Gene has a son too, but apparently the boy's not up to the mark."

Poor old Ralph. He thought he had the universe by the scruff of the neck. He'd been getting worse, too. He'd recently started wearing obsolete teenage clobber. A stylized version anyway. Flared pants with cuffs. Paisley shirts, purple more often than not. Stuff like that. And it wasn't only clothes. When he climbed into these hideous threads, his manner somersaulted. He became 'groovy'. It was a prickly business for the onlooker. 'Ralph Messer, symbol of progress and tolerance.' That's what you were supposed to see. It wasn't easy. What I saw was an ignorant smirk between brand new sideburns. They're what did it, I think, those bristly grey sideburns.

"Mr Messer, I think I'll finish up next Wednesday."

When I knocked off that day, I took a spin along the river. My twelve-dollar bike was still holding out. I crossed the bridge at Punt Road, heading north. Plenty of action had come my way in *this* part of town. Not that I missed the Wayne Turbills of the world, the undercover cops, but at least I'd *felt* something in those days. Since I'd been working at the factory, everything had blurred together. Well, I'd now dumped the factory. And I knew I'd leave Fitzroy too. Shelley could get someone else, or not. Plenty of cheques were coming to her from Lloyd. Letters too. His band was finishing off an album. They'd been in the studio for weeks.

Some of my lyrics were being used. There'd be royalties, according to Shelley. I'd have to be patient. Record companies weren't known for their efficiency. Or their honesty — that was *my* guess. I wasn't holding my breath. I had no contract anyway. Even if they did cough up, I'd still be at Lloyd's mercy. And hippie etiquette was flexible. He might split his fee, or he might not... It looked like Shelley had completely abandoned the idea of singing. She'd even got a T.V. to stick in her room. Mexico didn't mind. They both sat glued to it. They studied it together. They were learning about obedience. It was no good to *me*. Our laughs had petered out.

My game plan was taking shape. For a start, I'd try and duck the rent cycle — I'd get hold of a sleeping bag, a classy one. It would be worth it. Like a real estate investment. I'd never be stuck. If I happened to find shelter, great. If not, I could deal with the elements. But I wouldn't be derelict. I'd still be calling the shots. There'd be no scratching at kitchen doors. None of that nonsense. I'd feed myself, as always. Living on bread and water wouldn't bother me. As long as I didn't have to waste any more time.

When I rode up to the house, three figures were perching on our verandah. On the old couch. They were strangers. Two girls, maybe sixteen or so, and a bearded guy dressed in white. Indian shirt and stuff. I introduced myself. The girls stared through me. One of them reached out, like she wanted to touch my face or something. The bloke got down on his knees and put his forehead to the ground. I'd seen this kind of routine before. They were trippers. Acid heads.

I went inside to find Shelley. She and Mexico were in the yard with three other people. More strangers. Shelley was pointing a long feather at the sky. Her guests had pots of paint. They were slapping it all over the statue, the giant lady. Mexico was in on it too, splashing the feet with scarlet. Shelley was nodding and smiling. It was no time for making banal enquiries. Or giving my notice. I went back inside, and up to my room.

The two girls from the verandah were in there. One of them had my bike tipped upside down. She was spinning its wheels. Her mate stood in a corner, laughing and crying. Through the window I could see the guy in white. He was still down on all fours. I decided to go out for a walk. The guy in white must have heard the gate. He called me back, and whispered in my ear. He wondered whether I'd ever *really* seen a bull-ant.

Part 3

No one met me. No one expected me in Adelaide. I'd finished work the previous week. Sunday, I'd left Shelley's house and gone straight to the station. My bike and blankets I'd left behind. I'd chucked out my worst clothes. I was down to my rucksack and a lightweight sleeping bag. I'd got it right at last.

I'd spend a month at Mum and Dad's, writing songs. After Christmas, probably Sydney. I'd never been there, for one thing. And maybe I'd find Simon. His room in The Rocks was my only clue. The rundown I'd sent him of the Gilbert and McQueenie Show had been our last contact. No response in five months. Mr Mordecai knew nothing either. He'd halved Simon's allowance. The rest he was stashing for later. I hadn't seen much of him since we'd fixed up Bartos, but we'd spoken on the phone. He was pretty worried. But he'd let Simon deal with his own tangles. What choice did he have? He'd promised to forward any letters that arrived for me.

I guess Monday's tiresome in most cities. I wouldn't judge Adelaide by its present glum manner. In fact, I wouldn't let it touch me at all. I'd see Mum and Dad, spend a month with my notebook, and get out. Simple.

The streets here were so wide and empty. That's what struck me. In three years I'd forgotten the backwater tone. But something felt different. On the train there'd been a couple of headbands. Bare feet had met them on the platform. A nationwide drifters' network had been established by this time. I guess no town was exempt. You couldn't say Adelaide had turned cosmopolitan, but it had rubbed its eyes. And maybe stretched.

I headed off on foot. The parklands were the same. And the freight yards. A few vacant lots had appeared in our suburb. I couldn't remember what had stood on them before. Except one. The old quilt factory on our corner had gone. Its rubble still covered the block. I wondered about the squatters, the Munchkins, but not for long. I spotted Mum standing at our gate. She hadn't seen me. I ran. I didn't want any long distance stuff. Nothing rowdy. I got right up to her.

"Mum!"

"Hello dear. I'm deciding whether to go and see Mrs Davey. You remember her, don't you?" Mum indicated the house directly opposite. "Mr Davey's been retrenched. I don't know what they'll do... "

Et cetera. Like I'd only been gone for a couple of hours. Mum kept talking, getting onto various topics, all locally based. But her eyes didn't glaze over. She'd improved in some ways.

"How's Dad?" I ventured at a suitable gap.

"...I don't like to say it, Wanda, but I think he's entered his second childhood. He's been attending these, you know, the Vietnam marches."

I couldn't believe it. I hadn't even been on a demo myself for ages. In fact, not since I'd left Adelaide. I guess I'd figured my presence wouldn't make any difference. I knew these gatherings had grown huge. They weren't just beards and sandals any more. But Dad? I couldn't get a grip on it. I hadn't replied, and Mum had kept talking.

"...Your father thinks he can become a soybean producer just like that!"

"Dad's quit his job?"

"Not yet, but he's been talking about it for weeks. I know what caused it. That jolly Morris has filled your father's head with rot."

"Morris?"

"I don't like to say it about God's creatures, but this man is despicable. He must be forty if he's a day, but he's got the long hair, and the scruffy clothes... I'm afraid he's a hippie, Wanda. I don't know how he got the job in Dad's section. Perhaps he wore a cap... He's interested in motor-cycles. That was enough for your father. Now they're firm friends."

"Since when?"

"Oh, two months at least."

Our letters had thinned out. There'd been nothing either way since midwinter. This Morris business probably wouldn't have been mentioned anyway. It didn't qualify as a worthy subject. There was no point in pressing Mum for details. I'd get plenty later from the horse's mouth.

I mentioned that I'd had one of my songs recorded, that there was an album in progress. Could I stay here till Christmas and work on new stuff?

"Of course, dear. What happened to your job?"

"The factory? I left."

"What will you do, Wanda? Are you going back to it?"

"No. I thought I might inspect Sydney."

"Sydney? But you've never been there!"

And so on.

Mum had work to do in the shed. Toy repairs. It was that time of year. She hadn't even started. She'd been too worried about Dad, and Mr Davey's retrenchment. My free-wheeling arrival probably hadn't helped either. I took my pack inside, and ran a bath. All sorts of forgotten trivia came to mind while I soaked. Not much of it amused me.

I got dressed and sat down straight away at my old homework desk. I had several songs that were half done. They just needed panel beating. I got right onto it. 'Nameless Dread' was one. I'd had it in pieces for months. No excuse now. I was right at the source. Finger on the pulse. I'd dash it off in an hour.

I did too. It was still only midday. This had been a good move. If I stuck to my guns, I'd have an album's worth of lyrics by the time I left for Sydney. I set a target — thirteen flawless gems. Shouldn't be too hard from the mountain of notes and outlines I had. Most of it in my head. Some crammed in the pocket of my rucksack. I figured a month-long burst should do it. Then I'd see about copyright and stuff. I'd been too slack. Lloyd held the purse-strings at the moment.

I wrestled with the scraps all afternoon. For some I had punchlines and no leadup. Elsewhere, verses fluttered around waiting for a hook. A couple clicked in one hit. Bang! There you are! Like a seance. Too easy. I couldn't bank on this happening every day. Most of it would be hard-fought. There'd be hours of staring at nothing, followed by a frenzied shuffle of words. And maybe a completely new angle by the time I filed it in the drawer. I knew all this. For ten years I'd been polishing the act. Counting my early fumbles that is.

At about four I packed it in for the day. Dad would be home soon. Mum's alarm at his rebirth, or whatever it was, had intrigued me. So had the idea of Morris, the forty-year-old hippie. A rare beast. Obviously Mum had met him. He must visit occasionally. I still couldn't imagine Dad being swayed in this way. Not that he'd ever bolted his mind against new stuff. Not at all. He wasn't like that. But at the same time, he was short on curiosity. Or had been, till now. His electrical dabblings and his motorbike had added up to a life. He hadn't cared to look out the window. I guess he'd been satisfied, that was one way of putting it. He'd never had any close friends before, either. He'd always got on okay with people, but liked being alone. Now there was Morris, and a blaze of great notions. Or something like that...

The gate no longer squeaked, but it scraped. I heard it from my room. I suddenly realized that I hadn't seen the old dog. I wouldn't ask. I ran out to the backyard. Dad had turned to flip the latch. His hair was collar-length and oil-free. There was no sign of a kitbag. A small rucksack hung on his shoulder. I called out, and he spun around. He had sideburns.

"Wanda! We thought you'd disappeared! Are you back for good?" There was a bit of hugging and stuff. I told Dad my plans. He got excited about my work. When would he hear my songs on the radio? I explained that Lloyd was still more or less smalltime. That the record was on a backyard label, that it probably wouldn't be played much in Australia, and so on. No matter. It existed, that was the point. Dad understood okay.

Mum came out of the shed. She'd lost track of time. She'd better start preparing tea. Dad waved his arms around. He never used to do that.

"No need! I almost forgot! Morris has invited us to his place. He's preparing a feast."

"I can imagine. But Wanda's here now — "

"The more the merrier! You really don't know Morris. He'll be pleased to have us all there. His brother Steve's bringing a few friends."

"But how can we... " Mum indicated the detached sidecar on the back porch.

"The bus. We don't have to stay all night. And someone might drive us back anyhow."

"Mr Free-and-easy! You're talking more like that man every day."

"Morris is alright. You'll like him, Wanda, I'm sure."

Mum took ages to get ready. She eventually came out in her pleats and fake pearls. I guess she was making a Statement. She wore a hat as well. Dad, on the other hand, had already appeared in a fringed waistcoat. He had a serene expression on his face, and kept nodding slowly. A couple of times he'd dug out his watch. It was the same old wristwatch, but now he kept it in his pocket.

Three abreast, we sauntered to the bus stop. Or maybe we Trucked, I'm not sure now...

Morris lived at a suburban beach. It was still light when

we got there. His weatherboard house stood on a double block. Every available patch had vegetables growing on it. Morris couldn't stand waste. Even Dad hadn't been here before. His face lit up when we found the joint. He knew how Morris lived, but only from his conversation. Here was the evidence. Mum was appalled. There was an enormous dove painted on the roof. Wind chimes tinkled near the wide open door. Joe Cocker music came from the back of the house. Dad walked straight in.

"Morris! It's me, brother."

Mum pulled a face. We followed Dad down the hall. Incense burned somewhere. Morris appeared from the kitchen. Flour covered his hands. He was bearded, with long curly blond hair, T-shirt, embroidered shorts. He nodded to Mum. Dad introduced me. I'd obviously been mentioned before. Morris put his fingertips together and leaned slightly forward in greeting. He seemed harmless enough. Mum bristled. We were led outside. A table was set up in the back yard. Lights were strung on forked sticks. It was a party, maybe thirty or forty people, all hipoid. Mum shuddered. She'd lost her nerve a bit since the days of feeding the quilt factory squatters. She probably regretted wearing pearls. But she kept her head up. She acknowledged everyone. I did too. No names were reeled off. Too much to remember. Waves and nods, that's all.

There were a couple of torn armchairs, and Mum perched on the edge of one. Dad sat on the lawn, legs crossed. Someone brought us drinks, apricot nectar and yogurt whipped together. I scoffed Mum's as well. Morris dragged Dad back to the kitchen. A lentil pie was maturing in the oven. Mum kept fidgeting. I stayed with her. I knew a bit about the Sore Thumb role. She'd need a safety net.

106

A girl came round with sunflower seeds. Mum couldn't be persuaded. To her it was parrot food. I took a handful. I asked Mum if she'd like to look around the garden. She jumped at it. But shouldn't we check with Morris? Dad's disreputable friend had suddenly become her anchor. The devil she knew, I guess. We went inside. Morris was tossing a salad. Dad was making himself useful, keeping an eye on the clock — the pie wasn't far off. Mum had already relaxed a bit. The garden tour no longer seemed necessary.

Morris talked as he worked… His friend Jill should be home soon. And his brother Steve was also due any minute. It was Steve's thirty-second birthday, hence the party.

"We didn't bring anything!" Mum in a panic.

"That's cool. No one cares about presents."

Morris was okay. Unlike many other hippies I'd met, he seemed at home in this kind of life. You didn't get the impression of amateur theatrics. He would have been about forty, like Mum had said. I wondered what he'd been like in his youth. No flower power back then. He'd probably looked the same as everyone else. But with saintly dreams lurking under his felt hat.

"Jill! Here you are… And Steve! Happy Birthday!"

The brothers hugged each other. We got formal introductions this time. Jill had a cheese-cloth dress and black hair in a long plait. And African jewels. Steve had the same sort of curly blond hair as Morris, but no beard. He wore a loose red shirt and tight jeans. He was clearly Far Out, but direct as well. Forceful even. A strange combination. Quite rare. He said he'd brought some people with him. They were already in the yard. They'd taken the side path to 'avoid hassles'.

Morris shooed us all out of the kitchen. He'd handle the pie and things on his own. The outside armchairs had been taken by the new arrivals, Steve's friends. He took us over to meet them. They seemed pretty stoned to me. And a bit edgy. Mum and Dad were probably mistaken for the drug squad. Steve soon patched up the gaps. A few words, a nod, maybe a joke, I can't remember exactly. But defences were dropped in no time. Even Mum was laughing now and then. Steve was a born M.C.

People fork out every day for etiquette books, set speeches, all kinds of tomfoolery. But you can't learn diplomacy. It's made of hunch and nerve. You find it in your cradle, or you do without. This guy could have run the show at any level. International intrigue would have been a board game to him. But he had other ideas for the moment. They soon came out. He had the rock'n'roll bug. He played drums with a band called Mojo Circus, a local affair with a reputation for disruption. Teen idols in other words. This partly explained his youthful entourage, but they obviously weren't just music fans. There was more to it. They seemed to hang on every syllable that Steve flung out, like he'd been to Hell and back, and could save them years of research. Something like that.

He was a guide, a sturdy rope, a trail of bread crumbs. Mainly, I think he was proof that you needn't be through at thirty. He wasn't tongue-tied either. He had a million stories, and he wanted them off his chest. There were motorbike yarns. He and Morris had been in a gang at some point. Dad was hooked at once. There was nothing technical, no fuel ratios, no boy talk. Steve didn't want to shut out half the audience. He kept track of the overall response. Any hint of a drift, and he'd lure the culprit back with a quick remark, tailor made. There were even Christian references for Mum. Because of her pearls, I guess. Anyway, you get the picture. It was mesmerism.

Morris and others had been loading up the table. Steve closed his chapter gracefully, and we shambled across to the banquet. The pie hogged the spotlight. It was two feet across at least, and a foot deep. Salads everywhere, and jugs of the yogurt drink. And oversized carrot cakes. Dried fruit too of course. And beans, mountains of beans. No one hesitated.

Most of the people would have been in their twenties, I'd say. Perhaps Morris and Steve didn't bother with old folks much. Dad had made it because of his Harley. It was better than a passport. It linked him up with a worldwide club. How he used the green light was his own affair. Right now he was ecstatic. Like someone about seventeen, wheel-standing through the school yard on the last day of term. That's how it looked to me. He was laughing and talking with all sorts of characters he would have dismissed in the old days. I wondered if he'd tried smoking anything. Probably not. I couldn't ask him of course.

There was feasting and conversation. Groups formed and broke up. There was loud chatter at the table. There were murmurs and giggling from the shadows. Daylight had gone. The coloured globes were good enough. But not for Steve. He'd rounded up his crew. They were piling up the makings. There'd be a bonfire. He took charge of the stereo as well. Apart from Joe Cocker, we'd had the Stones and Frank Zappa. Steve had brought a tape of Turkish music. Anyone else would have been howled down straight away. Not Steve. He stuck it on and the party stepped into overdrive. It sailed. I had to take my hat off. The guy was a kingpin. People even danced to these presumably unfamiliar rhythms. Steve lit the bonfire.

Mum and Dad were having a great time. A bloke with a Prince Valiant haircut was feeding them astrology. They wouldn't have bought a word, I don't suppose, but the guy had a child-like manner and endless enthusiasm. He made them answer questions. He drew attention to their glorious destiny. He was a good time Charlie. Infectious too. Not in Steve's class, but competent enough in the sideshow style. I strolled from one group to another. I browsed among the chatter. There was the Vietnam question. And revolution. More astrology of course... And Woodstock, what it may have meant, and so on. Organic gardening too. This bit was new to me, and I stuck around for an outline. Overall, though, it was merely the changing of the guards. I could see that a fresh bunch of platitudes would eventually ease the old into the gutter. There'd be a new code, policed in a new way. Independent thought would remain a stray dog.

I shook these morbid ideas, and looked around for Steve. I figured he'd stick to his guns, whatever happened. The bonfire had flared up, and most of the people were hovering near it. The Turkish music had run out, and no one had quite known how to replace it. I found Jill, and she told me Steve and his gang had gone out the front to get their drums. Apparently these kids were members of a percussion workshop that he ran. They reappeared from the side of the house with tambourines, castanets, all kinds of stuff. Steve had a pair of congas. He set them up, and plundered a chair from someone. He messed around with a key till he had the skin right. Then he spelt out a rhythmic pattern for his apprentices. None of them got lost. Steve

110

was a metronome. An educator. His power didn't stop at anecdotes. There was more dancing too. Stamping of feet, swaying arms... Do as thou wilt...

By midnight, only a skeleton staff held on. Steve, with a couple of his drummers, Mum and Dad, and me. Two or three others, but they were sleeping already. House guests. We'd lined up a lift with Steve. He had a bus, no shortage of room. Miles Davis played on the record machine. No one talked.

Mum and Dad were still laughing when we got home. Steve and Co. drove off. The bus was a diesel. It made plenty of racket.

* * *

Two weeks passed like nothing. I was on target. Nine songs were in order. I'd underpinned key lines and played down any padding. They looked sharp. Apart from a couple of sad ones, this collection dealt with freedom, staying aloft, dodging the traps et cetera. Old themes of course, but I had a few angles that might grab people. It was an age of curiosity.

Morris had called at the house a couple of times. Mum was getting used to him. I think she even liked him in a way. But she still regarded him as a potentially dangerous influence on Dad. It didn't take much to get Morris onto the subject of farming. And Dad was all ears. He was starting to calculate possibilities. The mortgage would be paid off soon, and then... Mum was horrified. She could see Dad losing everything on a breezy punt. Lychees, organic strawberries the size of apples, snow peas... And soybeans of course. These formed the staple of his new friend's dreams. Morris himself didn't have much to contribute. A bit of money, but no house to sell, nothing like that. He planned to round up other backers, and sniff out the right corner of Paradise. His brother Steve was flat out with music. Mud bricks weren't his cup of tea at the moment. But he liked the general idea. He'd do a bit of hustling. Fundraising.

I tried to imagine Dad out in the scrub, leaning on his Harley, bewitching a dozen raw Utopians with tales from the Dark Ages. Fun, of course, but not worth his life's savings. Or maybe it was. Maybe it was the best step he could take. I wasn't about to comment.

On the Sunday before Christmas I wrote to Shelley. We'd parted on sane terms and agreed to stay in touch. I'd done all I could with my thirteen songs. From Shelley I could get an update on Lloyd's moves, and plan my own accordingly. If he looked like stooging me on the stuff he already had, I'd find another market. If not, we could maybe draw up a deal. I could offer him complete lyrics for a second album. He wouldn't have to shop around.

Not long after I got back from the post box, Morris turned up with Steve. They'd brought a huge basket of vegetables that a friend had grown in the hills. This friend had coaxed his harvest from third rate soil, using various non-poisonous techniques. Anyone could do the same. A water source, a few bucks in reserve.

Motorbikes weren't mentioned that day. The Farm took on a life of its own. The brothers were obviously sincere, but this didn't mean their notions were tight. Mum kept pulling faces. She couldn't understand people choosing what she considered to be a Third World existence. Her own life was, of course, fairly humble, but at least the rain didn't drip on it. And a failed crop would touch Wall Street before it touched Mum. You could read all this in her frown. But she said nothing. There was no point lassooing Dad on the spot. He'd eventually get tired, he'd rest, he'd sleep on it. With any luck, he'd see the crazy aspect sooner or later. Why make trouble? Talk's cheap enough.

The time flew. Mum invited the visitors to stay for tea, but Steve had a Mojo Circus rehearsal at his house. Morris was to drive him home. Would I like to meet the band? Why not? It was Steve's main project. How could it be dull? Besides, they may need lyrics. I'd check the layout. I hadn't mentioned my work. In fact, I hadn't spoken to Steve at all yet. Not really. I'd listened.

It turned out that Steve and his band shared a house. There were other people there too, transients more or less. In short, a commune. The place had seven or eight bedrooms, including a couple of attics. Also a cellar. It was pretty rough. Ramshackle in fact. Within the next year or so, it was to be demolished. Meantime, the rent was laughable, a token. The Mojo bass player had lined up the deal through his father, an auctioneer. No lease of course. Three weeks' notice could bob up anytime. But until then the joint was a bird in the hand.

Morris dropped Steve and me at the gate. You could hear the band tuning up. They were in the cellar. We crunched along the driveway to the trapdoor, and Steve helped me down the stairs. They were steep, not much more than a ladder. I wondered how they got the amps and stuff in and out. There was a Hammond organ too, you couldn't stick *that* under your arm. Everything stopped when we appeared. Steve introduced me.

"Wanda, this is Art Haines, cult hero in residence."

"Hi, Wanda."

I don't think Art was pleased to see me. Or perhaps he wasn't used to being introduced. He was the guitarist.

"And Chris, and Noah."

Chris, the bass player, nodded and picked up a song list. Noah looked up from his keyboard and blinked. Steve sat down at the drum kit. The band's next performance was set for New Years Eve. Only a couple of weeks to sharpen up recent compositions. Art directed proceedings. He dealt out chord charts from a folder. I sat on the brick floor. Steve counted up to four with a stick. That was the last I heard of any percussion. What followed was essentially a volume battle between Art and Chris. Art had a bigger amp, but Chris was quite good at spotting loopholes. Noah ran up and down the organ keys, but wasn't in the hunt. The vocals also were missing in action. When the racket stopped, I made a trivial excuse, too smoky or something, and scrambled up the rungs. I knew roughly where I was and walked home. It took an hour and a half.

The next morning, Steve came around in his bus. He was off to the beach. Did I like swimming? He didn't seem to have been put out by my early exit from the band practice, my wordless critique. In fact, he seemed especially cheerful, as though he applauded my reaction. It was odd. Anyway, I grabbed a towel.

Steve knew a deserted spot south of town. No one to bother us about wearing bathers. A patch of freedom within commuting distance. It sounded okay. The bus was dark green and didn't attract too much attention. Steve drove it like an ordinary car, pouncing on opportunities every few seconds.

"Art was angry when you left last night."

"Angry? I got the idea I was unwelcome."

"That's not the point. You rejected a privilege. Rehearsals are private. Even the people living in the house leave us alone. I broke the rule taking you there, but that was nothing compared to *your* unprecedented move. No one walks out on Mojo Circus."

"Why *did* you take me there?"

"Well, to get acquainted. I thought we'd have a chance to talk."

"Talk?"

"Well, you know. After the practice. I thought you might have comments to make, on the music. Which you did, in a sense. Morris says you write songs. I thought — "

"Ah! Dad must have told him. I write lyrics. And they're not going to be drowned at birth by *those* spoonbills."

"No, no, I didn't mean that. We've got enough material. I just wanted your general view on the band, that's all."

"Well, now you know. Who does write your lyrics, anyway? And more importantly, why?"

"You're a cynic, Wanda. Our music doesn't always sound like that. On stage, everything's clear. You can hear every word. And even the organ sometimes."

"What does Moses think of having his music annihilated?"

"You mean Noah? I don't know what he thinks. He doesn't talk."

"What? he's a mute?"

"Well, no, not literally, but it comes to the same thing."

"Hmm. Anyway, who writes your lyrics?"

"Art. The music too. And it's all good. Come back to the

house later, and I'll play you a tape we made. The guy in the studio set up a muffling system. You can distinguish every note."

"A muffling system? Why didn't they just turn down?"

"Because they're twenty one, I guess. I don't know. It's a law of nature."

"And why did *you* get involved?"

"They were stuck, and I was available. I'm also the best. A fortunate coincidence. I don't know how long I'll stay. It's entertaining enough for now. On stage at least. The basement farce is part of the job. No one learns a thing down there. At our shows, everything's played on the wing. 'Fun Anarchy', that's how we describe the music. It's no secret. The fans lap it up."

I'd been handed my first clue to Steve's doctrine. He appeared to be a taster, a variety fiend. He was no Gibraltar. I'd better keep that in mind if I planned to get tangled in his life. Which I did...

No one was around. The beach was a blank page, like Steve had said. We stripped off and ran into the sea. It was pretty calm. Only a few minor waves crept past. We swam out to about neck depth, and floated and laughed. It was easy to imagine that the world had ended, that somehow we'd ducked under the net. Steve talked a lot, mostly about nature and survival. Spartan stuff. Romantic though, not preachy or anything. After that, we splashed around in the warm shallows for a while. When this seemed like nonsense we headed for the bus, and its silken sheets.

* * *

Christmas at home again. A bit strange. I'd spent the last few days at Steve's place. Mum and Dad knew, and were confused. It wasn't disapproval exactly. I wasn't a kid. But they wondered why I was getting caught up in something when I was supposed to be taking off for Sydney. It looked frivolous I guess. My response came to me on the spot. I was digging out a coin from my pudding. A genuine sixpence. You couldn't use the decimal stuff. A chemical reason I think. Or maybe it was superstition. I'm not sure. Anyway, I'd made my decision.

"I'm moving in with Steve. Sydney can wait."

This option had existed for two or three days. I'd been telling Steve 'Maybe'. Now, in his absence, I'd agreed. Mum and Dad were the first to know. They looked even more baffled, but I had nothing to add. I helped myself to more custard, and Mum started clearing the table. Dad probably felt responsible for everything. His contact with Morris had laid the foundation. He perhaps didn't really mind. Like many others, he'd been charmed by Steve. So had Mum, but to what extent I wasn't sure. Nor was Dad. He didn't know what to say. He didn't want any arguments with Mum about modern conventions. Certainly not at Christmas Dinner. He said nothing. Eventually we both got up and dried the dishes. Mum didn't say anything either.

Later in the afternoon Steve came past to pick me up. We'd arranged to visit Morris and Jill. I ran out to the gate when I heard the bus. I told him Okay, yes, I'd skip Sydney and live with him. Not the most glamorous setting, but better than Mum asking him, "What's all this?" before I'd got a word in. I took Steve into the house, and we had a beer with Dad. Mum had a shandy that coloured her world. Steve, as usual, knew what to say. In half an hour or less he was regarded as family. He dug into his shoulder bag and produced a bottle of perfume. Also 'Classic Motorcycles', a glossy opus with detailed notes. Both were tied with ribbon.

My hobo kit was already at Steve's. I left Mum and Dad's place empty-handed, but it was a change of address just the same. It was a honeymoon, if you wanted to get technical. The gears crunched, and Mum and Dad waved. I felt pretty weird. Like I was in one of those corny movies that people make for the money. But perspective soon returned. I'd made no deals. I was still free to bolt whenever I wanted. To Sydney or anywhere else. Steve was free too. We weren't mugs... We'd covered all this during the 'Maybe' stage.

There'd been no word of demolition. Winter had turned up, and plenty of rain. With any luck, we'd be able to crouch in the house till Spring. Pots littered many of the rooms, catching drops. But it was better than paying four times the rent elsewhere. We were surrounded by factories and warehouses. Rock'n'roll Heaven, no danger of a noise raid. For nearly six months I'd been copping the Mojo Circus rehearsals. They'd got louder if anything. I'd kept away from the cellar. They did sound better from inside the house. For one thing, you could hear the drums. Not in detail, but you knew they were present. I'd been to shows as well, of course. Nearly all of them. The band excelled before a crowd. It pulled something out of its hat, some foreign object only distantly related to the row they made down that hole.

Incidentally, I'd made a point of witnessing the roadies at work. Two giants they were. They'd reverse their truck up to the trapdoor and fill it in about ten minutes. They used hooks and ropes. Even the Hammond organ didn't worry them. They flipped it around like a card table. Specialists. Professionals. They did it for glory and a jug of beer. They called themselves 'Circus Hands', a title which had social clout, apparently. They didn't complain. What for? There was a queue of strong guys with similar ambitions.

It wasn't slavery. The band members sometimes got even less. Glory of course, but often neither money nor beer. Incompetence in business matters was a sign of Coolness. If you mumbled about cash, you had no place in rock'n'roll. Chris, the bass player, was the only Mojo who ever engaged in such vulgar discourse. He tormented the others with his banal claims. They'd shake their heads. Chris could play, but his attitude was haywire. He didn't understand tradition. This was the unspoken consensus.

Steve and I were still having a good time. He did stay out all night now and again. It was no surprise. It was part of the deal. I could do the same if I wanted. Overall, things were okay. The laughs outweighed the rest...

On stage, Steve called the shots. Not just musically. He always had a microphone, even though he didn't sing. His remarks kept the show on the boil. He could make crowds do anything. At one gig in the park, he stirred them into a frenzy, and sent them marching to Police Headquarters. He didn't leave the stage himself. You need drums to punctuate this type of caper. Anyway, off they went — students, hippies, reds, fists raised, and more or less in step. At least until they got out of earshot... Luckily, nothing happened. There were no bombs or rocks thrown. But they did march half a mile, and they did keep shouting. A lot of punch for one drummer boy. This was the beginning of Steve's 'Revolutionary Phase'.

From Jill, I heard about his other Phases. Stuff from the past. For instance, in his bike days with Morris, the ride itself hadn't been enough. There'd been all kinds of rituals too, some of them semi-criminal. Then, after a few months of this, he'd suddenly snapped out of it. Repentance he'd called it. He'd dumped his leather clobber, and entered a theological college. Again with all the trimmings. He'd parted his hair in the middle, and worn horn-rimmed specs of window glass. And the daggiest suit available. He'd shopped around. Everything had to be perfect. I couldn't help thinking of McQueenie, and his bizarre stunt, but at least in his case there'd been profit involved. Steve, on the other hand, couldn't have made a cracker on his little productions. It wasn't even theatre, really. He lived out these characters twenty four hours a day. Until he thought of a new one. I'd seen 'Hippie' and 'Revolutionary' so far. Very convincing. What next? I wondered.

Jill had felt obliged to warn me. Steve's changes weren't always as smooth as the one I'd witnessed. Hippie to Slogan Monger wasn't such a radical step. I should be prepared. That was the message. Steve had been a Sioux Warrior. Also an American Pioneer eager to open up the West at any cost. At one stage, he'd even worn a pair of fake six-guns. I thought for a moment that Jill was getting carried away. But I knew her by this time, and she wasn't really the type to spin yarns, or even exaggerate. I was entitled to this information. That was her angle. I appreciated the tip-off.

120

I'd never got to know the other Circus folk properly. Chris was always out. Art stayed in his room. I guess he'd conjured up a role for himself too — Prince in Exile. At least he stuck to it. Noah never talked. Ever. What was *his* part? Harpo Marx? Zorro's valet? You tell *me*.

There'd been no response from Shelley. Six months had passed since I'd written. I figured she'd forgotten me, and moved onto other scenes. But late in June, Dad dropped in with a large envelope that had turned up from Melbourne. He hardly ever came round. I occasionally visited him and Mum. Sometimes we'd see him at Morris and Jill's place. The farm project had been marking time. There was still plenty of talk, but nothing had materialized. Dad was willing to buy into something reasonable, but wouldn't be the stooge for a bunch of would-be sharecroppers. Morris was still chasing up other investors. And Steve made an enquiry now and then. But nothing happened. Maybe the verbalized dreaming was enough. Maybe they could do without their fertile valley...

Okay, the envelope. A couple of pages from Shelley, and another envelope, sealed and blank. I read the letter first. Apologies for the delay, she was caught up in this and that... Mexico was two years old. Lloyd was on a roll, had sent us copies of the record. She knew I'd like it.

I opened the smaller envelope. Apart from the album, there were royalties. A bank document, anyway. The guitar whizz had come good. Sales were going okay. Larger companies had shown interest in further recording. The band was holding out for the best deal. Here was a good faith cheque, there'd be more. Lloyd had also enclosed information about copyright, and a sample contract. Did I have further lyrics?

Yes, I did. My thirteen shanties were still snoozing in a wardrobe. I'd been slack, but this time it would pay off. I'd have to get onto a lawyer and sort out details. Action at last. $830 as it turned out. Steve had been paying the bills. I'd been considering factory work again. My thirteen songs, strangely enough, had been almost forgotten in the Mojo Circus whirl.

Steve usually had some kind of work outside the band. Sessions for instance. Sometimes jingles, but also demo tapes, or even records. Solo performers would often put scratch bands together for various one-offs. They had their pick of players, and frequently wanted Steve's drumming. These jobs paid properly. There was no rock'n'roll ethic here. You got your money, and that was that. It came in handy. Steve had spent time in the jazz world. He had plenty of contacts among players of his own age.

There was kind of a pool. Maybe a dozen regulars, who had the paying work sewn up. A couple of horn players, one or two other drummers, and so on. Probably enough to form two permanent outfits, plus someone on the bench. But they didn't do that. They mixed it up, they shared the spoils.

A few weeks after my windfall, a particularly rich offer was made to Steve and some of these other jazz guys. Namely, a tour of Vietnam, entertaining the troops. If anyone else in the rock world had even considered such a thing, it would have meant tar and feathers. But Steve was able to announce to the Circus that he'd be unavailable in September, and the first week of October. He recommended a ring-in, a fiery punk who'd recently joined his percussion workshop. And without hesitation, he told them where he'd be... No horror, no derision. Just a few

122

questions about the kid, the suggested substitute. Astonishing! What I found even more mysterious was the fact that Steve had even been selected for such a tour. There were other drummers of similar standing. Only two or three, but why pick the public agitator, the guy with the red star? The rules really didn't apply to Steve. There'd be no better proof than this. Okay, the authorities had asked him to have a haircut. Hardly a mammoth hitch.

Steve got his papers and injections. He rehearsed three or four times with the touring band. The apprentice came round for a run through with the Circus. His style didn't suit the music perfectly, but he would be okay for a fill-in. Steve went to the barber for a barely noticeable trim. Then he got his ticket and vanished.

You wouldn't think the captain's absence could make so much difference. Almost at once, the household started to slip. Things had always been casual, of course. It was a commune after all. But it had somehow kept afloat. Now it tottered, and fell in a heap. No one did any work. The simplest task was allowed to drift. I did my own share, but I wasn't about to pick up the pieces. By the fourth day, squalor had a firm grip.

The grapevine hadn't shrivelled either. All kinds of blank-eyed drifters floated in. They clearly weren't police. That was the bright side I guess. Acid casualties they looked like to me. They didn't greet you, they didn't even glance. They stared and shuffled. Bare feet and ponchoes filled the hall and kitchen. Even the cellar. A couple of twelve-year-olds curled up down there. Urchins, Queensland bound. They weren't sure when they'd leave. Maybe late Spring.

Faces changed I think, but the number of guests hovered around thirty. The scientifically placed pots had, of course, been disturbed. In the second week, I think it was, the rain muscled in as well. Everything squelched. The firewood had gone, and we just had to wear this new disaster. It frightened off several of the temporary residents — another silver lining. I'd breached etiquette by this time, I'd put a bolt on our door. I didn't leave the bedroom very often. One of the attics it was. Quite remote — a big plus.

I wrote to Lloyd after I'd had the contract checked. When everything was set up, I registered my stuff and sent him copies. I hadn't read through the songs because I tend to make changes. It was a bit late to do that properly. Besides, it was time to get into writing again. Maybe a third album for Lloyd, if he liked the current batch, and if the record company agreed, and if the band retained its perch near the top of the underground. Quite a few ifs. I felt lucky though. Well, professionally, anyway.

Junkies were burning the chairs and stuff. It was getting pretty desperate. Art had arranged for the roadies to look after the band equipment. The cellar waifs had been no threat, but we'd reached another level now. Siege I guess you'd call it. Another mob appeared when the weather improved. Then we got more rain. Wild eyes and dripping beards. Just like a newsreel. A bulletin from a strife-torn corner of the tropics. Fun Anarchy had seen merrier times...

I'd got used to the shuffling and cackling, and even the breaking glass. I could sleep through it all. But one night, a brand new racket woke me at about one o'clock. This time it was loud thumping. Someone kicking a door maybe. I got dressed and went down the stairs. I knew I probably wouldn't be able to do anything, but I was curious. By the time I got to the ground floor, I realized it was heavy boots stamping up and down the hall. A torch was flashing around. Sleepers were being kicked. There were yelps and swearing. A raid. I was a legal tenant. I shouted.

"What's going on?"

"Good question, Wanda!"

"Steve!"

I flicked on the light. There he was. G.I. Joe. Steve had grown six inches. He had a regulation haircut. His ears stuck out from under a cloth cap. Shirt and pants of camouflage material. Huge belt buckle. Huge gleaming boots. And some kind of short whip. He pushed me away.

"Lights, Wanda! All the lights!"

"Welcome home, Bilko. Do it yourself!"

I copped a stranger's glare. Steve had every right to be furious, but not at me. I couldn't have sorted this out on my own. The rest of the band hadn't cared, once the amps had been stashed. They wouldn't have backed me up. They would have called me warlord, or something like that, if I'd made a move against the invaders. Anyway, I'd kept out of things. It was done now. Maybe Steve would have better luck.

He switched on the lights. The rabble had stirred itself. The people who'd been kicked had gone already. Others now followed. Steve whacked them to shake any doubts.

"Yo! Let's go! Yo!"

That's what he said, over and over, until we had our house back. I don't know about the cellar. Hansel and Gretel had already left, I think. Anyway, there was no one down there by morning. Steve's feet must have been eloquent enough, I guess...

"Are the others here?" Steve meant the Circus.

"I suppose so."

He pounded on all their doors.

"Council! Council!" he shouted. "Chris! Art! Noah!"

Out they came, unshaven, wretched, half naked.

"Right, men! Broken glass to be placed here! Splintered furniture near the fireplace! Let's go! Yo!"

They weren't quick enough. Chris copped a flick on the ear. Steve stuck the whip in his belt and started work himself. He was demonic, pumped up. He showed them how. They weren't about to rebel against their human pendulum — they needed his talent, if nothing else. There was no provision for smoko in this man's army. I got into it as well as a volunteer. I didn't knit socks either. It was hard work, a month of devastation to be reversed. Steve suddenly stopped.

"Attention, men! Full enquiry my room, 10 a.m. Sharp! Dismiss!"

And off they went, the angry young cult figures. They were back in school. Except there was no sniggering. They didn't even look at each other. Steve and I went to bed. I think he regretted his outburst at me. But he stayed in character. He was the Drill Sergeant. It was a Phase. You don't muck around with Phases. I knew that much.

It took nearly a week to patch things up. There was no point attempting major repairs on a condemned house. But we made it liveable. The floor wouldn't dry till summer. We spread out newspapers. Steve and the others sprayed some kind of tar on the roof. A temporary measure. There probably wouldn't be much more rain. Warmer weather wasn't far off. A few weeks.

126

Steve had questioned the band members separately. Just for the exercise I guess — I'd given him the whole saga by that time. He'd reported to me afterwards. Art had said that none of it would have happened if the moon hadn't been in Capricorn. Something like that. Chris saw it as a lesson, an incentive — the Rolling Stones didn't have to witness such behaviour, unless they felt like indulging in it themselves. In which case they were able to pay the bill. Even Noah had said something. Not much. "The horror." That's all. He'd said it a couple of times, but hadn't elaborated. Steve and I had laughed. We'd both read Conrad. Noah couldn't invent a thing. Maybe a riff or two that would never be heard.

Steve had refused to practise until the work had been done. The others were obviously concerned about his new image. It didn't fit their manifesto at all. The stand-in drummer had done a good job, playing three or four gigs. But he couldn't be regarded as permanent staff. Maybe after a couple of years he'd be up to scratch. In two weeks, there was a big university show to be played. Steve's hair would still be spiky. And he wore a uniform all the time. He had three identical jungle outfits. Not real, of course, he hadn't joined up, but he was more military than many who had. No one was about to take him aside and offer him a wig... He was still in charge of a unit. He was whipping the Circus into shape.

During his second week back, Morris came around. Steve hadn't even phoned, and there were fears for his safety. Morris laughed straight out. He was the big brother after all. Steve drove him from the yard with his whip. Morris left quietly. He was laughing too much to resist. This small event turned the tide. Everyone had seen it. I kept a poker-face, but the others mocked him openly when he came back into the house. Steve was shaking. He busted the whip over his knee, and chucked the pieces into the fireplace. We heard the bus start up.

He didn't come back that day. Or the next. I was worried. And angry. Why couldn't they leave his Phase alone? They only had to play along. The hard part was over, the mop-up detail. Rising at dawn for a few more weeks wouldn't have killed them. And Morris wouldn't have had any duties at all. Why had they been so impatient?

I didn't sleep the second night. At first light, pigeons crowded the gutters as usual, cooing and scraping around. I heard one of the factories starting to hum quietly. It seemed too early for that. Then I remembered it was Sunday. They shouldn't have been working at all. I went to the window. I couldn't see much. The sawtooth roofs, nothing else. The humming came and went. I remained puzzled. I narrowed down the source to the base of our one and only tree. Eventually, I made out a light-coloured patch. I waited, making guesses and rejecting them. Finally I had to take it on the chin. It was a kaftan. It was Steve, with a completely bald head, and a brass Buddha at his feet. He was sitting cross-legged. I called out. The humming didn't change at first. Then it became 'OMMMMM...' drawn out for nearly a minute.

I took a deep breath. Several, probably. I tried to rationalize. "Okay," I said. Maybe out loud, I'm not sure. "Okay. Let's say you're not only a hippie, but a public figure, a rock drummer due on stage. There's been a brief but terrible gap, during which you've had your hair hacked off. Not by military police, or a prison barber. There's no heroic aspect, it's not a sacrifice, it's not martyrdom. You sat in the chair and gave the word. You volunteered. Then you revved up your mind to the appropriate pitch. You had people bluffed for a while, you had them jumping. Then laughter came. The worst possible reaction, the one invincible comeback...

The jig is up. You have to dump the role at once. But how? Beards are optional. Collar-length hair is acceptable for neophytes. But you must have *something*. There are no exceptions to *this* rule. Even if you're known and respected, you can't just fling the ensign overboard. You can't just sell out with complete impunity. Of course not. And you can't grow a foot of hair in a fortnight either. A tricky spot. But wait! The fans haven't seen you in uniform. Hardly anyone has. The bleary-eyed squatters don't count. There's an option. A bold and precarious one. All the better. You've transcended long hair! You've left hippiedom far behind! You're a leader once again! You've turned Monk! Of course! Of course!"

I had Steve's number. I was sure of it. He'd ride this out like everything else. In entertaining fashion, no doubt. He'd at least be consistent in that respect.

I got dressed and ran downstairs. Naturally, the household slept on. No one knew the Sergeant had returned. Well, he hadn't anyway. I ran up to the still life. It kept humming. I wasn't sure of protocol. I suddenly realized there wouldn't be any, except 'Keep your distance'.

Monasteries are strictly gentlemen only. I stopped in my tracks. Steve slowly opened his eyes. He looked at me as though I were some curious tourist. Then he nodded slightly towards my feet. I looked down and saw a straight line made up of carefully placed leaves. I understood. I froze. Then I backed off. A tough new Phase had begun. But there was no use in arguing. Celibacy would prevail. I gave it a month. Steve would have maybe an inch of hair by then. He'd think of something. He always did.

Art and Chris had to live with it. For the moment at least, they'd have another clam on stage — Steve wouldn't be requiring a microphone for the present. The fans also bought the monk routine. Outside of bellicosity, Mojo Circus could pull any stunt it liked. Steve actually shaved his head completely a couple more times. Then he left a strip in the middle for a day or two. This was then honed down to a modest top-knot, soon to be put out of its misery by another full shave. Then Nature was allowed to take over. The Mohawk and the top-knot had been desperate, uncertain variations. There'd been no sartorial back-up. They were stabs in the dark. 'Cries for help' they'd be called now. In those days, they were just patches of hair…

When there was finally enough to work with, Steve went to the barber. He came home with slightly shorter sides, and spiky stuff left on top. It was still too soon for curls. The kaftan was gone. He had loose, pleated trousers, and a white shirt. He was a 'Hipster'. A world-weary jazzman from the late fifties. You could see straight off that he'd jammed with Dizzy Gillespie. And had probably met Kerouac in a little-known diner. He talked, of course.

'Greetings bro,' he said to Art, and taught him a special handshake. The pressure was off. Buddha wouldn't be mentioned, but at least we'd find out what had happened to the bus.

Another Christmas came and went. So did a couple of royalty cheques. We spent them like it was shore leave. Steve was getting plenty of studio work. Mojo Circus, on the other hand, was staring at ruin. The magic had faded, the gigs had dried up. There'd been nothing since New Year's Eve. It was now mid-February, '72. We had to be out of the house by the end of the month. We'd had a good run, longer than any of us had expected. Steve had retrieved the bus. Even in his spiritual fervour, he'd had the wit to stash it with someone. An old friend, a mechanic. It was running like a watch. I must admit, I wouldn't have been surprised if the sergeant/monk had nudged it off a bridge, with his wallet as chaser. But there it stood, the trusted beast. We wouldn't be stuck for a roof.

Steve's curls had returned, and he'd grown a goatee. Other props included striped T-shirts and sandals. He drew the line at a beret. Between 'Hipster' and 'Beatnik', he'd gone a bit preppy. He'd shown a photo of JFK to the hairdresser. The guy had shaken his head in despair. "We're not magicians, mate." Steve had settled for a Garfunkel crimp, but it hadn't survived the first wash. Overall, these changes had been made with grace and authority.

A couple of decisions had to be reached quickly, and were. Mojo Circus would fold. A four-way split. And there'd be no more house-sharing either. It was curtains. Bad luck and everything, but the facts were blatant. Time, gentlemen, please!

The farm talk had been flaring again. Not from Dad's corner. He'd got rid of his sideburns, and returned to his solo meditations in the back shed. He only saw Morris at work. They hadn't fought, or anything like that. They'd drifted. Dad was Dad, as he'd suddenly remembered. It was no big deal. Morris, though, had finally aroused interest among a few acquaintances of his own age. They'd agreed to fork out, if he could find the right patch of land. They were on the edge of hippiedom. They wanted to burst right in, and they had the fare. There was nothing tying them down. Anywhere in the country would do, provided there was potential for subsistence. They wouldn't scramble in the dirt getting whacked on mushrooms. They were grownups with families. Their attitude was a lot like Dad's had been a few months back.

Morris realized this enthusiasm wouldn't last forever. He would have to start hunting for a property. Not so easy. Northern New South Wales seemed to be the best bet. Communes had already started to spring up in that area. It should be checked out first. But Morris couldn't afford to blow his modest nest-egg on a scouting trip. His laughter at his brother's Drill Sergeant phase had been long forgotten, and he now asked Steve and me to help him out — we could drive the bus, keep our eyes open, take photos, ask questions, and so on.

Presumptuous perhaps, but not crazy. We had a few hundred bucks between us, and no urgent commitments. Steve could do ad sessions if necessary, in Sydney. He wasn't nationally famous, but his name was certainly well-known inside the profession. I had another string of half-baked songs. I was lucky. I could work anywhere. My thirteen songs had been accepted. Knobs were being twiddled already — Lloyd's second album would appear in the northern summer. There'd be proper money then, if it took off.

I'd only had four of my works on the previous record. Its sales had been quite good, but were now levelling off. I probably couldn't expect much more from that source. Lloyd had promised me advance royalties on Album II. Out of his own pocket maybe, I wasn't sure. Anyway, he'd come good before, and I didn't doubt his word.

I'd have to keep producing though, if I wanted to have another batch ready. Lloyd III perhaps, if his bubble didn't pop. Otherwise, I'd have to hustle around. That would be okay too. I had plenty of confidence by this time.

As for the pilgrimage east, why not?

* * *

It didn't matter what sort of junk was abandoned. We didn't have to clean up the joint. Everything would be dust before long. A bulldozer, a few trips to the dump, and Mojo's headquarters would be forgotten, along with its apparently immortal performances. There were no regrets. Bands go through stuff like this all the time. You knew the odds at your first sound check. No use bitching if your nag tumbles. No one made you gamble.

Steve left his drums and furniture with Morris. And his old costumes, the ones that couldn't be adapted to the present mood. Right now it was Back to the Land. This meant overalls and cotton shirts. The goatee was being extended into a Quaker-type beard. It would take two or three weeks to look right. That was okay. We'd decided on the coast road. We'd pay our respects to Melbourne and Sydney. We'd dawdle, we'd keep a lookout on the way up north. Eventually we'd plant our banner in the Promised Land. We'd phone Morris. Nothing to it.

Lloyd had come good with a small advance royalty. We'd be able to side-step trouble for a while, and have a laugh or two. And contact friends here and there. Shelley for instance. And Mr Mordecai. And Simon? Maybe. I wouldn't hold my breath. It was nearly two years since Bartos, and all that stuff. A long stretch. It seemed like an old fable now. Some yarn I'd glanced at in a waiting room.

The first leg was easy. A picnic. A leisurely cruise through familiar territory. We'd driven southeast several times before. Mostly for the spin. Once with the band — The Circus had booked a tin shed somewhere, stuck up posters, packed them in. 'Top Adelaide Band. One night only'. That kind of thing. It had been simple. Isolation still meant something in the early seventies. People starved out there.

The coast was different. Steve's bus wasn't huge, but it shouldn't have stepped onto this kind of track. We had to keep hugging the cliffs when cars appeared on the ocean side. We got dirty looks. It wasn't fun. Just a jagged rhythm, a stop and start routine that drained us. Not all the time though. Dancing on the edge had its moments. We weren't thinking about agriculture yet. The latitude was wrong. It took nearly three days to reach the outskirts of Melbourne.

It was late in the evening when we arrived. Steve knew someone at Footscray. We'd go there first. We'd surprise Shelley the next day. We found the friend's address, and pulled into the driveway.

"Not there! Not there! Who's that?"

An old guy in boxer shorts was shouting from the front door. Steve backed out and parked in the street.

"We should have phoned him, Wanda. This man can be

difficult. Don't question his ravings, whatever you do. He gets carried away sometimes." Coming from Steve, the warning counted. I had our host pegged already as a complete psycho.

"Dim your lights! You'll frighten them off! Who is it?" The bloke was really shouting. He was now standing at the front gate, still in his underwear.

"Calm down, Dredge. It's Steve. Can we stay the night?"

"I don't know."

"What are you talking about? Just say. We can go to a caravan park."

"It isn't up to me. There may not be a night. It's *their* decision." And so on. I wasn't in the mood for riddles. Anyway, Dredge took us into the house. He made peppermint tea. Then he made us listen. All kinds of nonsense. No shortage of tangents either. You couldn't get hold of a thread anywhere. We were sitting on the floor, beneath a dazzling fluoro. There was no furniture in the room. I wondered if he even had beds. Sleep was all I cared about. But Dredge kept ranting, and striding up and down. He had a caged globe on the end of a cord, like mechanics use. Every now and then, he turned off the main light, and swung this thing in a circle, while glaring up at a tiny skylight. Then he'd switch it off again, and the fluoro back on. None of this upset his flow of words. There was stuff about cosmic rescue, and purity, and someone he was expecting from Atlantis. I was nodding off. So was Steve.

"Over here! Over here!" I woke suddenly. Dredge was flashing the globe and letting the cord out as he swung it, making a kind of spiral. Steve hadn't stirred. It was getting a bit cold, but I must have dozed again anyway. The next time I woke shivering. Dredge wasn't around. It was dark, except for the now grey skylight. I found the light switch. I shook Steve, and shut down his questions. We got out of the house, and took the bus to a spot near the racetrack.

The peak hour traffic soon disturbed us. I didn't care. We'd be able to reach Carlton in a few minutes. My old standby. The Lygon Street cure. Caffeine with pageantry, not much to ask. We cut across the top, past the zoo. We parked in Drummond Street and walked. I felt light-headed but sharp. We floated around for an hour or two. We scoffed cakes, and eavesdropped, and laughed. There'd been minor changes here and there, but it was still Carlton.

We strolled back to the bus. Kids were climbing on it. They poked their tongues out and ran off. Steve chuckled. He was starting to look pretty homely with his new beard. It wasn't quite long enough yet, but you could get the idea. He looked like he didn't belong in the city. I figured we should really be horse-drawn. I didn't point this out. The bus had been hemmed in a bit. Steve wrestled with the steering wheel, and we aimed at Fitzroy. It was late enough for Shelley to be up. The old house had paper daisies gummed to the front door. No one answered for a long time. I called out, and a curtain moved. Then a bit of racket, and the door opened. A guy about eighteen, wrapped in a sheet. "G'day. Does Shelley Moss still live here?"

"There was a Shelley." Good. I guess we didn't look like cops.

"Mid twenties, red hair?"

"Yeah, but she's gone."

"Do you know where?"

"Abbotsford."

"Have you got an address?"

"Shelley said not to…"

"Is she on the phone?"

"Yeah, but…"

"How about you giving her a call, and saying Wanda's in town?"

"We've been disconnected."

"How about I give you ten bucks, and you hand over the address?"

He pretended to hesitate. An ethical gesture.

"Okay, I'll see if I can find it. Have you got a pen?"

"Here you are."

The guy paddled off to the kitchen. I could see him copying something off the wall.

"Where's the cash?"

We got back in the bus and took off. We'd made that kid's day. I didn't know the street he'd given us. We got hold of a city map, and tracked it down. The area was mainly industrial. There weren't many numbers visible. It was starting to feel like a bum steer. We parked the bus. It was a bit tricky to manoeuvre in these alleys. Plus we'd see more on foot. We covered what seemed to be the general vicinity. Then I saw 'Moss Icons' on a brass plate. Second floor, it said. There was only a goods lift. We climbed the stairs and rang. The door opened straight away.

"Wanda! Good Lord!"

We hugged and laughed. I introduced Steve, and Shelley ushered us into her studio. She called it a space. Her long hair was gone. Only about an inch remained. And she had little specs with gold frames. You'd have to say she looked urbane. Especially next to Steve. She was already taking us on a tour. The northern wall had glass louvres. A big sloping work table stood near it. Sketches were scattered everywhere. On the other walls too, tacked up in rows. There were two doors at one end of the room.

"That one leads to our living space. Mexico's at the

babysitter's. She'll be three in June, a real chatterbox... But I'll show you the engine room first. Then we'll have coffee."

Shelley opened the other door, and led us down a corridor into a much bigger area. She'd rented the whole top floor. In this part, five or six people were bent over trestle-tables, drawing and ruling lines.

"My wonderful staff! Kids, I'd like you to meet an old friend of mine, Wanda...and Steve."

The kids looked up. They weren't all kids. One lady would have been about thirty. They nodded and smiled, and got back to work. Their jobs suited them. You didn't get any hint of clock watching. Shelley led us back to the first room, and through to her flat.

"I work in here too, as you can see." Sure enough. Draped statues. Shelley had certainly graduated from Simon's garage. I wondered if she'd ever cleaned up the giant woman that the acid heads had covered in paint. I wouldn't ask. We'd never discussed that incident. She put the coffee on, and approached the sculptures.

"These are in transition. I'll show you though." She quickly whipped off all the covers. I got the same sort of blast as the first time, when I'd been snooping around at South Yarra. Four years it was now. My old mate was absent, but these three weren't so different. Maybe they'd even been carved from the pencil-marked blocks I'd seen.

"Shelley, they're great!"

"Ha! They will be. This is my personal project. The kids have their work, I have mine."

"They look finished to me."

"No, no, you haven't seen — wait a moment. Remember your favourite? The piece we had at Fitzroy?"

"Of course." She must have repaired the damage.

"Follow me. Steve, keep an eye on the coffee, will you? Through here, Wanda." Shelley took me into her bedroom.

"Voila! Behold, Our Lady of the Velodrome." There was my old pal. Still covered in paint, odd colours slapped on at random. But there'd been extensions too. She had a leather cycling helmet, and handlebars sticking out of her hips. They were off my old bike. I recognized the grips.

"Shelley!"

"You like? She's untitled, actually. Gene came up with the Velodrome thing."

"Gene Mordecai?"

"Yes."

"You still see him?"

"Not very often. We ran into each other at a gallery a while back, and I invited him to my first exhibition. That was in August."

"And he came?"

"He certainly did. He brought a friend too. Between them, they launched my career. Gene bought a whole stack of etchings that I did years ago. I hadn't planned to show them. But the walls looked rather bare. My newer work at that stage... Well, there wasn't as much as I'd hoped. A few months' worth. I started not long after your departure."

"You didn't say anything in your letter."

"Yes, well... I wasn't confident then. The exhibition changed everything. The friend bought Our Lady here. In fact, that's when Gene coined the phrase. He was quite open about it. 'Leonard! For three grand, you buy a second car!' You know how he talks."

"Three thousand dollars?"

"Yes. And by the time this chap takes delivery, he'll already have made a profit — fingers crossed! I was unknown then..."

"Now you're famous?"

"Not quite, Wanda. But I've seen enough to recognize a trend. Anyway, my buyer in this case is a respected dealer. He's in Japan at the moment. Leonard knows what's what. I set up my little workroom on his advice. Those kids are no slouches, either. I pay them top dollar. We're a happy family."

"What are they doing, though?"

"Designing...what you might call knick-knacks, but it's a little more chic than that. Decorative objects, some of them mobile, some static."

"But they don't have any function?"

"Good Lord, no. That's Rule One... They're focal points."

"Who buys them?"

"Aha! Good question. Everyone, I hope. Production begins next month. Contracts are being drawn up with manufacturers, and I'll farm out the work according to the medium. Most of it will be plastic. Nostalgia won't last... We'd better go back to your friend."

"He'll be okay... Shelley, how have you — "

"Credit, my dear. Let's have coffee."

Steve had already set up the brew. He was flicking through a magazine. Ties and Cadillacs and aftershave peered back at him. Hmm. With any luck, we'd get the crops in before a Beau Brummel phase took hold. Shelley filled the cups. I had another question.

"No word of Simon?"

"Simon? Nothing. I know Gene's worried sick, but as

140

you're aware, he wouldn't cry on anyone's shoulder. He just waits and waits. 'My son, the Invisible Man,' he says occasionally. You know...with that sad smile."

Steve looked up. He knew the story.

"We'll track him in Sydney." He had no personal interest of course, but even in the role of Saintly Serf, his curiosity was intact I guess.

"You two are going to Sydney?"

"We'll be passing through. My brother wants to buy land for a commune... Eden awaits our arrival."

"Well, yes. Quite... Have you had breakfast? Can I get you both something?"

"No thanks, Shelley. Our bread's already been provided for today." Also pastry, and foreign newspapers, but I wouldn't split hairs. Maybe Steve had really forgotten Lygon Street. I still hadn't plumbed the exact depth of his Phases. We finished off the coffee. I hadn't got round to mentioning Lloyd, or my songs. Shelley was obviously keen to resume her work. We muddled through the ritual — Must fly... Regards to Mexico... et cetera.

We drove down to St Kilda to visit someone Steve knew. No one answered the door. I was glad. I was still having flashes of Dredge, and his tangled fantasies of the previous night. I realized it was absurd to bundle Steve's friends into one basket, but still, I didn't feel like meeting anyone. We strolled past Luna Park and down to the beach. We didn't talk much. We paddled in the froth, and stared at clouds and people. We were taking it pretty easy for pilgrims. Showers came in off the sea, and we raced back to the bus. It was already afternoon. The rain kept pounding on the roof. We watched it trickle down the windscreen.

141

"Steve, I'll phone Simon's father."

"Okay." I found a booth, and got through easily.

"Wanda! You're back! When can we meet?"

"I'll be leaving again tomorrow, Mr Mordecai."

"Tomorrow? Then it's obvious. Tonight, you'll be my dinner guest. Name a restaurant."

"Thank you, but I'm not alone. My friend Steve...from Adelaide — "

"Bring your friend. I never thanked you properly for your help with that crook, that impostor. You've had word from my son?"

"No, I haven't. Shelley said you've heard nothing either."

"You saw Shelley? *There's* a dynamo. Some of her work is beautiful. The rest... Well, I'm not qualified to say. Tonight we'll talk. Where?"

I was anticipating a juggling act. Commerce meets Nature Boy. I'd be playing the go-between, a full time job... I didn't want toffs watching me clutch at the wrong fork. Nor brutes abusing Mr Mordecai.

"How about Capurso's Bar, in Carlton?"

"I'll book. Eight o'clock? Good. See you then, Wanda."

The rain had stopped. Steve was standing at the curb dipping his toe in the flooded gutter. It looked like fun. Another day perhaps. I didn't really want to slip into kid mode. I'd have to stay on the ball. Our meeting with Mr Mordecai would be tricky enough, with Steve liable to change gears at any moment.

"Steve. We're dining out. Mr Mordecai's invited us."

"I was thinking of fasting for two or three days."

"Start tomorrow. He's invited us both. I suggested Capurso's."

"Where's that?"

"Carlton. You'll like it. How about we take a room now, and clean up?"

We crossed town, and found a middle-priced hotel. Steve did the talking, just in case. They wouldn't say 'No Blacks', but they could make it awkward. As it happened, the clerk was indifferent. I guess racial diversity's no big deal in Brunswick. We climbed up to our room and showered. Steve set his travel clock. Dredge's late night antics had caught up with us...

The alarm woke us just before seven. I still had no fancy clothes. Jeans and stuff, that's all. I thought Steve would only have overalls, but I'd forgotten Special Occasions. Out came a quiet three-piece suit, and shiny boots. And a collarless white shirt. He laid them on the bed and went to the basin with his razor. The stubble came off his upper lip, making the rest of his beard stand out more. On with the clobber. He did his shirt up right to the neck. A modest chain gleamed on his waistcoat. He was prim. He'd gone too far if anything. Even the tired clerk looked twice when we passed the desk. And not at me.

Steve's Old Values manner stole the show... The guy at Capurso's didn't blink. We were guests, full stop. He ran a finger down his booking list, but I spotted Mr Mordecai, already seated at a table. He waved to us. He looked pretty sharp. There was a bit of grey in his beard, but otherwise no apparent change. I'd half expected signs of crumbling, from his ordeal with Simon. Steve and I crossed the room.

"Wanda You look well. And this is?"

"Steve Alexander. Mr Mordecai."

"Gene, if you please. How are you, Steve?"

They shook hands properly. There was none of that power-play stuff that blokes do sometimes. No crushing of fingers, or fighting over the top spot. No eyeballing either. Civilised it was. The waiter hovered around with his pad and pencil.

"Wanda? Steve? Something to start?"

"Maybe a beer, thanks."

"A beer? And Steve?"

"I'll have a beer too, thanks, Gene."

I was relieved. I'd thought Steve might order warm milk or something, to fit the costume. I guess his diplomatic instinct had prevailed.

"So, Wanda. A flying visit you say. How's Adelaide?"

"It's okay. Steve and I are on a mission. We're going to Sydney tomorrow, then — "

"You'll find Simon?"

"No. Well, we'll try of course, but that's not the mission. We're on the lookout for a property. Farming land."

"Farming? A mighty profession. Noble. And...you're buying? You and Steve?"

"It's for my brother and his friends. They're starting up a community. If we find a suitable spot, that is."

"Ah! Hippie communes. I've heard about such things. Can they really function? I wonder. In Israel they do, more or less. Not hippies of course. Hard work for its own sake, a different approach entirely. But they *are* communes. Your brother, he's used to work?"

"He's used to factory work. One of his partners grew up on a sheep station, but otherwise they're city people who've had enough."

"You'll need more — Ah! Thank you, thank you!" The guy had turned up with the drinks.

"Need more what, Gene? You were saying — "

"... Ah yes! Your city farmers. You'll need more than a wish to retreat from commercial life. You'll need dedication, endless practical knowledge, and preferably twenty six hours a day if you can swing it. I know about these things. You think I've never dreamt of a rural paradise? Everyone does, sooner or later. But you must eat. Hammocks and folk-singing, why not? But you must eat. And this means plenty of sweat. And early nights. And you must eject fressers at once — you know, freeloaders. People who slip under the tent, contribute nothing, demand food, usually in a tone that implies guilt on *your* part.

"Forgive me, I don't know where your sympathies lie, but it seems to me that this hippie business is based on such an attitude. 'Something for nothing' seems to be their philosophy — If it deserves such a title. They speak as if the figs grew wild. Well, no doubt they do in some places, but not where you find hippies. Such types want variety, and drugs and stereos. Something to fill their eternal holiday. If you ask them to help sow a field, you're a tyrant, you're the worst prick who ever walked! Forgive me. I've had this row before with people. With my son, in fact. Not in relation to agriculture, but the same argument nonetheless…"

He picked up his beer. He looked a bit worried. Because of Simon, no doubt. I tried to steer him back on track.

"No one's after a free ride, Mr Mordecai. It's a serious project."

"You two. You're planning to work this property?"

"We'll help establish it, Gene. And yes, we'll continue to assist for a while."

"What's your profession, Steve? If you don't mind my asking."

"I'm a musician. A percussionist."

"The South Australian Symphony! Then you must know my friend —"

"No, not that sort of percussion. I play jazz and rock. And sometimes I run workshops."

"Ah! I see. Forgive me, I thought — "

"The dark suit? No, no. Anyway, music's on hold at the moment, Gene. For me, at least. Wanda keeps plugging away."

"Wanda! You're a musician? You've never said."

"I've been writing a few songs, Mr Mordecai. Lyrics."

"Lyrics! I *knew* you were talented, Wanda. I hinted as much, yes? And these songs... You have people?"

"Yeah, some have been recorded. Others are in the works. Do you know Clearspots? The American band?"

"No, I'm sorry, I don't, Wanda. This is rock music?"

"Yeah, more or less. Shelley's husband, Lloyd, formed Clearspots about two years back."

"Ah! Shelley's husband. In America?"

"Yes, he was born there. He and Shelley used to play together in San Francisco. Shelley sang. That was before Mexico arrived."

"Shelley's a singer? All these secrets. Anyhow, good luck with your songs, Wanda. Well done."

Another waiter had come up. We hadn't even looked at the menu. Five minutes? Certainly. We scanned the options...

"Tell me, Steve. When you resume playing music, how much work do you expect to find in the country?"

"Hah! I've hung up my sticks, Gene. All I've brought is one small Pakistani drum. I don't expect to make a musical living. We'll be farmers. Or itinerant workers really. It won't be *our* place. Besides, the first step is to find somewhere."

"Of course, yes... Do you normally survive by playing?

You've always been a professional?"

"Mostly. But I've done a bit of selling, off and on."

"I thought so. You understand people. More precisely, you understand the individual. Am I right?"

"It's not for me to say, Gene."

"Of course not. Forgive my presumption — Ah yes! Are we ready to order?"

The waiter scribbled down our wishes... And more drinks? He'd send someone...

"I used to be a salesman, Steve. I don't know if Wanda's told you, I'm head of — "

"Bliss Bars Inc."

"Ha! Yes, quite. But when I was young, my father wanted me to learn as many aspects as possible — He was the founder of the company. There were some business studies of course. But he also made sure of my personal involvement in the various stages of production and distribution. You're laughing, Wanda. Yes, I did have your old job for a while. The packing room. Father insisted. He didn't want me bobbing on the surface. That's what he used to say.

"The machinery, of course, I didn't touch. Too dangerous if you're not properly trained. But every other job, Father insisted. Sales in particular. Two years I travelled. Country areas. Interstate sometimes. I was nearly thirty before I was allowed to make executive decisions... The war years of course had slowed things down, but even so. I tried to interest my own son in a similar path. Wanda knows how much luck I've had."

"I've told Steve about Simon, Mr Mordecai. Why don't you just get someone to check on him? One of your reps."

"I've tried that, Wanda. I still send an allowance, but

147

Simon's moved. A year ago at least. He's made some kind of arrangement with the landlord. A forwarding address, I suppose. But the man's sworn to secrecy. I'm not prepared to, you know, out-bribe my own son, as it were."

"But you wouldn't have to. Just hire a — "

"Detective? Yes, I know. It must appear strange. Everyday I pick up the phone. I still have that chap's card. Gilbert. I'm sure he's capable, but... I musn't weaken. What I should do is to stop sending money. I can't go that far, but at least I can leave Simon to his own decisions. This I must learn."

I didn't know what to say. Another round of drinks arrived. We nursed them in silence for a while. The restaurant was packed. I slipped into my fly-on-the-wall routine, checking people out. Steve was doing the same, I think. Mr Mordecai stared at his beer. It wasn't an awkward situation, but I knew it could be soon...

"We'll snoop around, Mr Mordecai. We'll be in Sydney for a couple of days or more. I don't know what we can do. Maybe leave our contact number with this landlord. Worth a try."

"I'd appreciate it, Wanda. I don't want to interfere with him, just..."

"We'll get onto it, Gene. Stop worrying."

"Thank you, Steve. It's not so easy being a father. Not when they grow up. You can't toss them in the air any more... Wanda, tell me about Shelley. You went to see her?"

"Yeah, this morning. She's certainly changed, Mr Mordecai. I know you only met her briefly back in the old days. But when I left for Adelaide, I thought she'd given up. T.V. and more T.V. It's all she did. No music. Certainly no suggestion that she'd return to sculpture… except… Maybe I shouldn't say, but I will. You know the piece that your friend bought?"

"Ha! His *Tour de France!* Did Shelley tell you about that? Leonard was furious when I laughed. He called me a Philistine, but I couldn't help it. Ha! Handlebars it's got! And Shelley has so much talent. I bought some of her proper work. Etchings they were. They didn't interest Leonard in the slightest. He's an expert, he must seek different things I suppose. I'm sorry, Wanda, I interrupted…"

"It's okay. I first saw that statue in Simon's garage. Without the paint and accessories. I couldn't take my eyes off it. We had it at Fitzroy too. Maybe you didn't look outside… Anyway, a bunch of kids painted it. Hippies. And Mexico too. She must have been about eighteen months old…"

The giggles overtook me. I tried to explain the before and after versions to Steve. It wasn't easy. I guess you had to *be* there…

"Hippies you say? Hippie art? Leonard must know! Ha! Ha! Ha! He *will* know!"

Mr Mordecai roared and slapped the table. Customers stared. The head waiter too. I'd been through this before, laughing in public. It's no use trying to stop. Anything you try to tell yourself makes it worse. Steve started chuckling as well. At Mr Mordecai and me, probably. I knew no one would throw us out, but we tried to tone it down a bit.

"The handlebars came off my old bike. Please don't tell your Leonard."

Mr Mordecai stared straight ahead for about two seconds. At first I thought he was going to cry. Then he cracked up again. He was hysterical this time. His eyes got bigger, and he coughed and laughed at the same time. Steve and I were off again too. I guess the head waiter had no choice. He came over and spoke quietly to us. Our food appeared at the same time. We sobered up. We swerved back into relative sanity. We started twirling our spaghetti, trying not to look at each other. The place buzzed. It was quite rowdy. I realized how loud we must have been for anyone to have even noticed. Our freakish appearance had no doubt contributed. An Aboriginal girl with her missionary and a business titan. An intriguing spectacle, I had to admit. There'd be plenty of guesswork…

We ate slowly. Steve finished first. He didn't rock the boat. In fact, he guided us to very dry land. Statistics.

"Gene. A question. Has there been a downturn in chocolate sales over the last, say, three years?"

Mr Mordecai looked surprised. Probably not by the enquiry so much as its source. I was baffled too. And alarmed. I thought Steve might be changing hats right in front of us. But it wasn't that.

"A downturn? What makes you ask?"

"Well, it's only a guess. I don't suppose the people I know represent a cross-section by any means, but there seems to be a growing tendency toward… you know, nuts and berries. Vegetarianism, macrobiotics, and so forth are becoming increasingly popular…"

"There hasn't been a fall in sales, but, let's say the growth is less steep. Possible reasons have been suggested, reasons much like yours. Originally, I snorted. A passing fad, I thought. I gave it six months. That was, from memory, in September 1970. The first gentle hint came about then. Barely discernible. Lately, I must admit, I've been a little uncomfortable."

150

"Maybe it's time to start churning out alfalfa sticks."

"Ha! Well, yes, I've certainly considered it. A simple enough thing, but... I've never had to jump onto a bandwagon before... This health craze stems, of course, from hippie doctrine. From a medical viewpoint, your nuts and berries are no doubt valid. But I suspect the appeal lies not so much in that, as in the idea that all you need grows on trees. Yes, obviously people pay for health food, just as they pay for anything else, but at the back of their minds, I'm sure they imagine they could trek out to the sticks and live comfortably without effort...

"I'm not accusing you two or your friends of that naive mistake, but it happens. You've perhaps witnessed people actually attempting such a thing. Or maybe you've heard of examples... Well, this kind of fantasy doesn't amount to much in itself, but it means advertising will have to become that little bit more sneaky. There are hints of it already, in some areas. Ha! Note these concepts — Freedom. Nature. Escape... Perhaps even Revolution. Advertising will be using such notions widely and profitably for many years to come. You just watch. The ad people will have to be careful to remain one step ahead, and *one step only*. The days of striding forth on a whim, and dragging the public by its ear, those days are gone. You watch. The next few years..."

Mr Mordecai hadn't touched on his actual plans, but even so, he'd been pretty open about things. It's usually greenhorns who behave like that. Absolute beginners unloading their enthusiasm. In this case, it must have been from a sense of commercial infallibility. Or boundless confidence, anyway. Whatever it was, Steve had been paying close attention.

"One step ahead, you say. I suppose that's near enough for sales purposes… But do you think it's possible to actually enter someone else's mind, and have a look round?"

"Someone else's mind? No, of course not."

"I know a guy who's spent his whole life trying to do exactly that. He's still trying, in fact."

"How? How can this be possible?"

"This guy tries to transform himself into everybody else. Not into specific individuals, admittedly, but he does cover a large number of psychological types. And he thrives on contradiction. Where possible, he will leap from one extreme standpoint to its opposite in one step. And it's not just a mental exercise either. His dress, his voice, his general manner take radical turns overnight. It started in childhood, apparently, but all kids jump on and off various fads, and no one took much notice. When he reached adolescence, he made a point of keeping on the move. This enabled him to leave his personality in a railway locker, so to speak. New scene, new character. Sometimes a new name. He didn't want to confuse or alienate people, and travel solved this problem for a while. These days he tends to stay put, and his audience just has to wear the changes. A certain number slouch away scratching their heads. Others are more curious, and stick around for the show… What do you think of this lifestyle?"

"Lifestyle? It's a puppet theatre. Your friend is unwell."

Steve just sat there with a wooden expression. The mention of a puppet theatre may have opened up new worlds for him. Who knows what he was thinking. Perhaps he was designing a strait-jacket. I didn't feel like asking. Mr Mordecai also waited quietly. The drinks guy came past, and I got another round. Steve took a sip.

"Gene. This guy is rational. Also, his behaviour isn't as irregular as you might think."

"What? Everyone lives in a cartoon? Is that your idea?"

"Nearly everyone, yes."

"Qualify, please."

"Essentially, he's doing what most people do. The only difference lies in the frequency of his actions. Others select a role model at an early age, start rehearsals, arrive at a clumsy facsimile, and remain there forever. Even outwardly varied lives usually adhere to this principle. My friend, by contrast, makes this kind of decision at least twice a year. What's more, his eye for detail is flawless. You'll never catch him in the wrong shoes, unless there's a particular reason to promote an apparent oversight. But apart from this meticulous aspect, he's only doing *repeatedly* what everyone else does *once*. The sole difference lies in this repetition. He has more energy than most, that's all."

"So. If I cube normality, I arrive at this friend. Am I close?"

"Close enough."

"But what a strange thing to do to one's life."

"It leads to expertise."

"Pardon?"

"It makes him an expert in dealing with people whose lives he's already experienced."

"I see... Tell me, Steve. How does he select his archetypes?"

"Books and films. Or if he wants something with a lighter touch, he may go to a bus depot, or some such place, and keep his eyes open till he finds a definitive type, whereupon he'll begin his preparation without delay. It can take hours, of course. Or he may keep seeing people he's already been, and have to try again the next day. But don't forget his opposites, his counterweights. More often than not, one character will suggest a sequel... For instance...

"Maybe rough thug to Buddhist monk."

"Thank you Wanda. Yes, that kind of thing."

"My dear young friends, I am speechless."

We all were for several minutes... Okay. I'd copped the backstage tour. I knew a bit more about Steve's mind. But a third person confession is near enough to worthless. I still wouldn't be able to address the Phases in any sort of open discussion. I'd still have to deal with the Tinker or the Tailor, whatever happened to surface. I still couldn't laugh. I'd have to continue playing along. There didn't seem to have been any point in Steve's flipping his cards in this manner. Maybe it was all just table talk, an impulse, nothing in particular. It was no good to *me*, anyway... Further nonsense suddenly emerged.

"I've made a calculation, Gene. My friend would have to live at least two hundred years to make any headway. That's without all the new possibilities that continue to evolve... Endless combinations."

"Yes, well. Good luck to him... I wonder if you'll find Simon. He'll respond to you, Wanda, I'm sure. Steve, my son tends to leap into roles, he may interest you. Unfortunately, there's not much of a spectrum, though. He invariably picks the loser's part. And he's always hunted, or thinks he is. A peculiar boy, I must acknowledge... Please find him. You'll both try, won't you?"

"Of course, Mr Mordecai. But if we have no luck, you must contact Gilbert. He knows his job. He nailed Bartos, don't forget."

"How could I forget? Ha! Bartos. Another player of games... Let's see how you go, shall we? Write to me at once, whatever the outcome."

"Yes, of course. We'll do what we can."

"... I think I should go, my friends. I know it's quite early, but I have work to finish off tonight... And I keep thinking about Simon. It can't be much fun for you."

"We've had a great time, Mr Mordecai. Thank you for everything."

"Yes. Thanks Gene. I hope my story didn't upset you."

"Your friend? I don't think he'll threaten civilization, do you?"

Eventually we stood up. Mr Mordecai and Steve shook hands again as we edged over to the door. Steve offered to 'pay for the drinks at least', but was howled down. Outside, Mr Mordecai reminded us once more about looking for Simon. Then we parted. Steve didn't talk on the drive back to Brunswick. He may have regretted spilling the beans, I don't know. I didn't care either way. I'd lost interest for the moment. Thoughts of Sydney were crowding my head.

Part 4

A simple rule prevailed in those days. Hitchhikers were there to be picked up. Only the most coarse reptile failed to jam on the brakes. That wasn't us. And we had plenty of room too. The road from Adelaide to Melbourne had been deserted. No applicants at all. But we were certainly prepared for our public service. No one stood in the elements if *we* could help it...

We'd got away from the hotel early, and decided to take the short road. I think Seymour is about sixty miles out of Melbourne. When we left its main street, it was probably about nine o'clock. A few miles further on, we spotted our first customer, squatting on the dry grass. He'd no doubt heard us ages before. Now he stood up and stuck his arm out. Buses were good percentage shots, like Kombi vans. Hippie vehicles. They tended to pull up. Our client was grinning, and tossing his hair back. He knew the traditions. We knew our lines.

"Where to, brother?"

"Sydney, eh."

"You got it."

"Thanks, man." He climbed over into the back, and flopped down on the bed. We took off, and grilled him for a while... He was supposed to be back at university in New Zealand. He'd been here for the summer, bumming around. He'd lost track of time and money. Luckily, he still had just enough cash for an airfare out of Sydney. In a couple of days, he'd be back in his home town. Willington, I think it was, some name like that. We gave him an outline of our mission. He knew about communes. He'd visited several, including a few north of Sydney, near the border... It was the best spot. He'd like to be rich. He'd buy land up there for sure... The kid was snoring inside the first hour.

We thundered along. The engine was loud, but regular. I could easily have slept myself. We made coffee stops to keep sharp, and took caffeine tablets to make sure. Steve sat up like a ramrod. He wasn't about to wipe out any fences — He was on the job...

There was still no chatter between us. The kid hadn't stirred either. I'd woken up properly, but kept daydreaming. I wondered about our chances of finding Simon. I didn't fool myself. If he'd wanted to contact me, something would have shown up via the factory. During my employment there, I'd kept thinking it would. But it was now well over a year since I'd left. Simon must have been pretty angry about Operation Gilbert to have clammed up so tightly. And angry over Bartos. That was probably the worst part. Idols tend to hit the ground with a bump.

Angry at himself too. He'd been through the kind of scene that breeds cynicism overnight. It can spring up like a toadstool, startling friends and relatives. I couldn't really imagine Simon in that condition... But why guess? We'd see him, or we wouldn't. We only had one tattered trump to plonk down — a message to be left at his old room, a number for him to ring. I wouldn't hold my breath... We'd be staying at Bondi with a guy Steve knew. A colleague from his serious jazz period. We'd only be in town three or four days. Our land mission wouldn't keep forever.

I think I must have drifted off after all. I sat up when Steve pulled in for petrol and I hopped out for a stretch. It was a desolate spot. Our jetsetter woke up too. He staggered off to the toilet like a toddler at midnight. A bloke came out and filled the tank. He kept an eye on us. Our overalls didn't fool him. He knew we were city folk, and almost certainly armed. Scared and bitter, that's how he came across. I advised him to install an espresso machine, and maybe a salad bar. He didn't like my gags.

Our modern youth climbed back on his bunk. We got cokes and chocolate. Bliss Bars in fact. The first time I'd faced them since the packing room. We drove off waving to the petrol guy. He shouted something. 'Boong' I think. It didn't warrant a U-turn. He already had his cruel and unusual punishment.

The kid stayed awake this time. It was early afternoon. I kept glancing back. He'd half emptied his rucksack on the floor. It was like one of those magic acts — a guy comes out in a jumpsuit with the sleeves pushed up. In twenty minutes, the stage is covered in flowers and strips of silk. Rabbits too, of course, and maybe a fridge or a small car...

Well, our bloke wasn't in *that* league, but from a medium-sized hiking bag, he'd coaxed four pairs of embroidered jeans, spare thongs, Indian shirts in several colours, an I Ching set, two hardbacks on astrology, a Tarot deck, a rolled up garment of crushed velvet, and five or six packets of incense. And he was still down the mine.

Out came his African skullcaps and a blow-up mattress. Then pay dirt at last — a giant bag of wholemeal biscuits. He left everything else and offered them around. They were pretty good, I have to admit. But what kind of mind packs a rucksack at random like that? Every time I caught a glimpse of Boy Wonder and his cargo, I burst out laughing. I don't know what our globe-trotter thought. Steve remained dead-pan. He knew me by this time. 'No questions' was our policy...

We'd just left Albury. Steve saw them first. Two more seekers lounging on the roadside. He turned to our passenger.

"Straighten your tie, brother. We've got company."

The bus skidded slightly, and Steve backed up. There was a pimply guy about twenty, and his pregnant girlfriend. They were good and stoned, I'd say. Or maybe they'd disciplined themselves into permanent drowsiness. Their clothes looked home-made, and quasi-biblical. Both were grinning.

"Peace," they chorused, like twins in a psychological thriller.

"Merry Christmas," was Steve's response. It seemed to frighten them a bit. The girl recovered first.

"... Thanks a lot. We've been here all day. Thanks a lot. How far are you going?"

"Sydney, if that's any use to you."

"Far out." The guy was already bundling their stuff in. Our Student Prince had cleared the deck, more or less. The new chums crawled on board.

"Hi." Still no names. I wasn't going to push. We all had our Journeys. Today we'd crossed, that's all. I knew the rules. Names were for dole forms. Steve found first gear, and the mission resumed. Before long, our riders were all old pals, wolfing biscuits and mumbling together. Steve, appropriately enough, was focussed on the road. I knew I should have learnt to drive by this time. I'd been slack. Maybe at Shangri-la I'd give it a go... I turned to our guests.

"We'll be going to Bondi. Do you two live in Sydney?"

Mary and Joseph started giggling.

"I wouldn't have my child in Sydney if it were the last town on Earth."

"Ah. So you'll just be passing through?"

This time, the young father conjured up his nerve.

"Yep. We're going to Coffs Harbour first, then to stay with friends in the forest."

"A farm?"

"It will be, when the time's right."

"Ah."

"What birth sign are you?" Mary again.

I invented something. She wanted details. I only had a rough idea about the time and place of my debut. The missionaries had painted over that stuff back in the '50s. I improvised further. One of the student's horoscope books was already open on the floor, and the stargazer flicked through it. She knew her job alright. It took less than a minute...

160

"You grew up among strangers who under-estimated your insight. You've forgiven them. Your true life is about to begin. A sublime future lies at your feet, but you must be patient. Gifts shall be delivered unto you."

"Far out," I sobbed.

I wondered what she would have said to a guy like Ralph Messer, my old foreman at the factory. "You will exhaust your days at street level. Expect nothing. Don't wait up." Ha! Not very likely.

"Your first kid?" I ventured. Someone had to break the spell.

"Yes. And there'll be no doctors. I'll squat in one of the rivers. It's not till July, though."

"Cancer," Joseph added.

Or frostbite, I thought.

"Cool," I said.

I returned to the comparatively gritty task of gazing at the scenery. The radio was our only chance of finding out the time. I scooted along the dial. No luck. We were in the bush alright. The surrounding terrain didn't appeal to me much. Nor to Steve, it seemed. Neither of us commented on the occasional 'Land for Sale' board that flashed past. Not that it was our decision anyway. We were only scouts. But it was generally understood that 'Back to the Land' meant wilderness, rather than the sort of isolation to be found in dry plains, or in established farming communities. We didn't slow down...

I didn't feel like starting up another chat with our honeymooners, but I wondered what kind of scene awaited them in the North. I knew it must be sub-tropical up there. Rain-forest and so on. Maybe their friends had just buried themselves in the tangled growth, and taken possession.

Found a cave perhaps. Even if you bought such land straight out, it would be a primitive and demanding life at first. Communal vigour would have to find its peak pretty quickly, and maintain it... Ha!

I remembered the situation at the old Mojo house, during Steve's absence. 'Something for Nothing' had indeed been the unwritten motto above *that* door. No building instinct had prevailed there. Was it a fair comparison? I didn't know. Perhaps not. Besides, it wasn't really our business. Steve and I might stick around with Morris for a few weeks, break the soil, erect a shelter of some kind. Beyond this, I couldn't imagine either of us getting caught up in such a closed circle. Steve's antics would be limited to three or four stock characters from rustic mythology. And I would run out of candidates for my hidden camera stuff, my eavesdropping, or whatever it was I'd always done. Anthropology! That's what it was, if anyone should ask. And how long would I hang around with Steve, anyway? It was still fun, despite his perversity, but it was no Darby and Joan set-up. We'd never be discussing each other's funeral arrangements, I knew that.

Silence ruled in the back of the bus. I took a gander. They'd all dozed off. They looked completely innocent. They trusted us. And rightly so, in those simple times. Thoughts of butchery and shallow graves occurred only to the most paranoid. Parents, and people like that... Steve's knuckles were white, and he didn't blink. His foot was heavy. It was mid-afternoon. We passed the Dog-on-the-tuckerbox near Gundagai. I remembered the song from my childhood. I knew I should use this time to come up with a few lyrics. Something to build on later. Steve and the sleepers re-

minded me of a real bus, a Greyhound or something...
Magical Mystery Tour had been done. Maybe that subject
was exhausted, I certainly was. Guests had the dormitory.
I snoozed sitting up.

"Wanda, do you want to see Canberra?" Steve was
whispering.

"Is this it?"

"No, we're just topping up. There's a turn-off not far
down the road."

"A turn-off? No, let's go to Sydney. What's this place?"

"Yass."

"... Let's go to Sydney. Have they got a clock?"

"It's about five-thirty. Maybe we should wake the kids."

"Nah. When will we get to Sydney?"

"Probably about ten or so. You don't want to go to
Canberra? — Wanda?"

...I dreamt that Steve held political power. He wasn't a
prominent figure, but he made big decisions. He was busy
at a typewriter, inventing new laws. Strange ones. From
the 1st of July, no one would be allowed to cling to an old
personality. Your appearance didn't matter so much.
There was informality in that area. But your tone and
manner had to change. Your thoughts too, strictly speaking, but this, of course, would be difficult to police.
Things like vocab, however, would be carefully scruti-
nized. Any hint of poetic expression would lay you open
to various charges yet to be determined. The aim was to
have everyone speaking like the Public Service Gazette
within three years. It was the most grotesque form of
tyranny imaginable.

I woke up suddenly and glared at Steve. He looked the
same as before. Of *course* he did. How could such a

repellent state of affairs have seemed real? It was absurd. I decided to try and stay awake.

"Where are we?"

"About ten minutes out of Yass. I thought you'd curled up for the evening."

"Nah. Did you get a drink?"

"Yeah, just behind your seat. Coke or ginger ale."

I groped around and took what came.

"This guy at Bondi's not a weirdo, is he?"

"Hah! You mean does he resemble Dredge? No, he doesn't. Far from it. He plays the world's squawkiest tenor, but if you saw him in the street, you'd say 'bank officer'. Which he is, by day. And he's about my age, so I don't suppose he'll ever let it go now. You should see him on stage though. Maybe that safety valve's enough. *He* must think so, anyhow."

"What did he say when you phoned him? Do you think it's okay to flop there?"

"Yeah, no problem. He was pleased."

"When did you last see him?"

"Oh, a couple of years ago. He came to Adelaide and stayed at my shack in the hills. Just before I moved in with the Circus it was. Hah! He was on long service leave. I couldn't believe it. Ten years in one gig. Nick's okay though. Harmless."

"Good."

This double-life type had always intrigued me. Jekyll and Hyde stuff, without the bloodshed. It wasn't Stevery, there was nothing fickle about it. Or even theatrical, really. It was more like a delicate house of cards. I'd had a small taste of it myself in a way, when I'd worked at the factory without abandoning my songwriting. But six months isn't ten years. And it certainly isn't a lifetime. It's hard to guess how widespread this twin existence thing is. Maybe thousands of artists prefer it to Bohemia. Thousands of people, perhaps with immense talent in some cases, who draw the line at staking their food and shelter. And it may not be faint-heartedness, either. It must take a particular kind of nerve to juggle with your stability like this, without losing the plot. Anyway, I'd have him under the microscope before long, this Nick…

We didn't stop at Goulburn. Steve's jaw was set, and his eyes wide open. I think he'd swallowed quite a few pills by this time. The sun had gone. I heard stirring noises in the back. Our scholar poked his head between the front seats.

"I must have slept, eh."

"Yeah. I nodded off for a while myself. We're still a few hours away from Sydney."

There were three or four biscuits left, and we knocked them off. The kid was bright-eyed, almost bubbly.

"Do you want me to drive, man?"

"No, it's okay. I'm awake. And these gears are tricky. I'd rather do the wrestling myself. Thanks anyway."

"That's cool. Did you say you're going to Bondi?"

"Bondi, yeah."

"I've got a place where I can stay in Glebe. Do you know where that is?"

"Yeah, we can drop you there."

"Thanks."

"What about the others? Did they mention a destination?"

"In Sydney? No. They'll probably just keep moving, I'd

say. You'll be going north, won't you?"

"Not for a few days. I can drop them at Central if it's not too late for a train."

"Have you been up the coast before?"

"Only as far as Newcastle. Where were these communes you visited?"

"Mostly around Mullumbimby. I met a girl in Sydney, and she took me up there. Anyone's welcome, it's really cool, eh."

"What sort of landscape is it?"

"Lots of jungle. They say it's hard to get the dole though. You might have to work sometimes."

"Is that so?" The dash light was on, and I could see Steve smirking.

"What are you studying at university?"

"Don't remind me. I flunked first year Medicine, and I've switched to Architecture. Dunno how it'll go."

"It's a good lurk, architecture."

"I'm not doing it for the money."

"What, then?"

"Dunno."

"Ah."

Steve let it go at that. It wasn't our business. The kid's opportunities were his to use, or dump under a bridge… I tampered with the radio again, and got something faint. Pre-Beatles pop. I put it out of its misery. The punk had a question.

"Don't you *like* music?"

"Yeah, but I'm fussy."

"Me too, eh. Do you like the Stones?"

"Of course."

"I'd love to play guitar."

"Why don't you?"

166

"Dunno. I should I s'pose. My old man's got a music shop. He'd let me have any instrument if I agreed to practise."

What a shameless clown. Imagine flashing *these* credentials. I don't think he even realized what he was saying. I felt embarrassed for him. How could you grow up in clover, and just blink at it? I looked straight ahead. Steve was chuckling. I guess he'd met more brats than I had. He got me off the hook.

"Tell me more about these communes. How are they run?"

"They're not run. They just *are*."

"Who sows the crops?"

"Everyone will, when they get it together. There's usually a few hassles."

"But you visited several places, didn't you? Tell me about one that's functional."

"What do you mean?"

"Well, surely there's been a harvest somewhere. You must have heard. How did it go?"

"It doesn't work like that. First you meditate. You can't just plant any old thing whenever you like."

"No, of course not. You mean these places have only recently kicked off, and plans are being finalised?"

"Sort of. One's been going eighteen months."

"And?"

"What?"

"Was there a bumper crop? Did people rejoice in song and dance?"

"What do you mean?"

And so on. Maybe Steve got a kick out of this drivel. It was no good to me. I even wished the others would wake up and reclaim their colleague. The kid was really starting to drive me nuts. But Steve kept egging him on with simpler and simpler questions. I had one of my own.

"Why don't you get some more sleep?" He took it at face value, but that was good enough. I heard him tossing around for a while. Then there was just the engine noise. The sky looked healthy. I stuck my head out the window. The air had cooled off. I sang one of my songs. Whispered it, anyway. I soon forgot about the Architect's Apprentice.

* * *

We'd stopped for coffee. It was Mittagong I think, or somewhere round there. The Prodigy woke up at once. He needed a leak. He and Steve made a dash for it. I called the other two. They must have been sleeping for about seven hours or so. They took their time getting a grip...

"Coffee break. Do you folks want to come in?"

"Would you bring us some milk?" Mary gave me a buck.

"Okay."

"Far out."

Steve had ordered. The Professor was still thinking it over. Perhaps white with sugar. I felt half-crazed. I just wanted to get to Sydney, and soak up whatever it had to offer. I strolled off to the toilet.

We knocked off the coffee and got out. I gave Mary the milk and change. She and Joseph needed to 'pay a visit'. That's what they said. They were sorry to be a nuisance. I tried the radio again. There was a guy talking rubbish, but the reception was good. I figured he'd play a record sooner or later. Mary and Joseph came back, and we took off. The DJ put on Van Morrison. Something off *Astral Weeks*. I jacked the volume up. Steve bounced in his seat. It wasn't far now.

168

When I'd first rumbled out of Adelaide, four years earlier, I'd been wide-eyed and gasping, with my tuppence ready. You could have sold me falcon's teeth and plastic jade. I was in the market, I couldn't wait to scramble onto all the rides. I hadn't needed a lot to have my head spun around. An Asian supermarket maybe, or a car parked crookedly on a teeming footpath. Nonchalance and vigour rubbing shoulders. Nothing much in themselves of course, but stuff that couldn't happen in the world I'd known previously, the world of dusty prudence and prohibition. No wonder Melbourne had blown me away, with its gleaming towers, and its dim chaos resolving into low-key elegance within a hundred yards, its arrogance and industry, and folksy fury passing comments in the crumbling slums...

But what about now? I'd heard a few jokes since then. I'd seen scams perfected and cancelled out. I'd met the leading actors of the day. Well, maybe not the leaders, but the best. A thousand times I'd misread scenes, and blinked and looked again, and picked up revelations crouching in the fog. I'd shaken punkhood, I was sure of that. Childhood had flapped its wings. But had I since grown weary? Had I seen the lot? Was I a dowager at not quite twenty three? I'd soon find out. Three million Sydney souls were lining up, awaiting their audition...

Steve wasn't mucking around. His eyes were even bigger, his foot heavier. The city had been in our sights for miles. And you could feel it too. It loomed up like a power station. We were still too far off to hear it humming, but that's what it was up too, you could tell. You didn't have to poke its biceps to know the score.

"It's big, eh." Our Lonesome Cowboy was peering through the windscreen. He'd seen the joint before, but maybe not from this angle. Signs of humanity were becoming more frequent. There were houses and shops and intersections, and the traffic started to feel different. Not slower. Everyone drove like Steve. But it was different, as if they all knew the turf, and weren't just intent on a speck in the distance, like the people on the highway had been. A buzzing urgency provided the drone. The rest was ad lib.

Quite suddenly, the impression of being out on the edge of something disappeared. There were used car yards and pubs. And light industry, and some not so light, and more car yards. We were in it now, sink or swim. The city centre, oddly enough, still seemed out of reach. It stood quietly, hands on hips and snorting. It seemed to be amused by the endless caravans bickering at its gates.

"I should change into my suit." This remark from Steve was no doubt intended as a kind of passport. As though I'd suddenly been admitted to the boardroom, after many patient months. But for once his timing was out. At that moment I had little interest in his foibles. I was full of this glittering and brutal town. It pumped me with adrenalin. It galvanized me, and tampered with my blood. It left me wordless, a chilling novelty. I'd just have to drop my jaw, and leave it at that.

The traffic roared. There didn't seem to be any rules, or even conventions. Except that you kept your foot down hard. It was a sprint. An evening at the dogs. The whole town bristled and stuck its chin out.

"Where to in Glebe?"

"Are we there?"

"Not quite. Have a look at this."

Steve plucked a street directory from a pocket in the door. Our Bantamweight found the light switch and the address without aid. He kept his finger on the spot, and stuck his head forward.

"Four more on the left. No. Three!"

Steve slowed down a bit, triggering an outcry from the traffic behind.

"Next one. The corner will do, thanks."

Steve turned anyway. There was no other means of pulling up. Our guy clutched his crammed swag and hopped out.

"Thanks a lot, eh."

"That's okay. Good luck in your career."

"Don't remind me. Thanks again."

We all waved. Steve manœuvred the bus to a strategic angle and grabbed the first gap. We soon got into step. There was a blues thing on the radio now. Junior Wells. Then the loudmouth returned. Even DJs have their uses though — we learnt that it was nearly eleven o'clock.

"Quo vadis, people?"

"What?"

"Where to? Sydney or the bush? I can drop you at the station, if you want to keep going. Get a train to... Hornsby, I think it is. You'd better check."

"Sounds good. Thanks."

We took them to Central. When they were gathering up their junk, they found the rolled up velvet belonging to the other guy.

"You'd better take it, kids. It must be an omen."

"Right."

They put their stuff down on the footpath. Joseph shook

out the new acquisition. It was a cape with stars and quarter-moons all over it.

"Far out," they agreed. We left them to it.

Steve drove off in a zigzag. We both laughed like maniacs. A passing cop glanced, but that was all. I figured the law in this town must have plenty of proper work to do.

"The Bridge!" Steve was like a kid.

"Is that the way to Nick's?"

"Right now it is." He couldn't stop laughing.

I'd caught a glimpse of the Harbour Bridge from some point back there, but the plot hadn't been blown. I still had no idea of its size and authority. In a couple of minutes I could see the whole set-up. I stared at its changing angles. Then we were treading its boards. Through the blurred bars the harbour lights winked. Cars tore past us. I leaned out the window and shouted as loud as I could. For as long as I could. At the other end, Steve turned off and took a back street.

"Shut your eyes, Wanda."

"Ha! Fat chance."

"You'll be glad. Or your money back."

I gave it a shot. There were more turns. And then more speed.

"Okay!"

I saw the entire throbbing city. We were back on the bridge, driving the opposite way. I was able to squeak out a sentence.

"People who don't live in Sydney must be unwell."

* * *

172

The sun appeared out of the Pacific. A new program for me. Nick's lights had been off the previous night, and we'd parked the bus at the end of his street. I'd slept okay till dawn, when I'd hopped out for a look around. Sunrise meant it was about six thirty, and I woke Steve. We'd agreed to call on Nick before he left for work. There was still a bit of time to spare. He wouldn't be up this early. We strolled down to the edge and paddled in the foam.

"What do you think, Steve? Shall we get a place here?"

"Hm. Maybe. We'd better finish what we started though."

"Of course. Say a month looking round up north, report to Morris, wash our hands of it."

"… Sounds alright."

"You don't sound alright, Steve. Don't you like Sydney?"

"Yeah, I like it. But a spin across the Bridge isn't the same thing as living here."

Steve had unearthed his jeans and denim shirt. His prison garb he called it. He looked kind of ordinary as he stood gazing back at the esplanade. I hadn't seen him in this get-up very often. It was a sign of his being in limbo. It worked like that bland ice-cream that toffs eat between courses, to neutralize the palate or something. What Steve's outfit amounted to was a tip-off. Denim meant that he might slip out to get a morning paper or a loaf of bread, and return in a tuxedo, or some such thing. On the other hand, it left him free to climb back into his overalls after a day or so. Maybe with a twig in his mouth, or wearing rubber boots. Some kind of reinforcement, anyway…

"Well, just say, Steve. I know you've made an arrangement with your brother, but after that? I'd like a clear picture, that's all."

"I don't know yet. Look, we'll be in town three or four days, right? Can't it wait till then at least?"

"Okay, fair enough."

We kept ambling along the sand for about ten minutes, and turned back. We didn't want to miss Nick. We'd park outside his house until there was a sign of life. I was content to stay with the original mission as far as our obligation went, but then? I was pretty sure I'd return to Sydney. Alone if I had to. There was no point in spelling this out now, though. I'd just have to wait.

Parking in front of Nick's wasn't so easy. We drove up and down his street, and wound up leaving the bus pretty close to where it had been. A futile business. I should at least have jumped out with our bags. Anyway, by the time we'd tramped back to the house, the front door was open. We rang the bell.

"Just a moment!"

Nick appeared. His face was covered with shaving cream. Part of one cheek had been scraped. He had a dark red dressing gown.

"Steve!"

"How's the man for whom Adolphe Sax invented the horn?"

"You stole that line. It was applied to Coleman Hawkins, or one of those guys."

"Good work, Nick. You're up early. This is Wanda."

"Hi, Wanda."

"G'day Nick."

"Come in, people. Put the kettle on. I'll finish my routine."

Steve found cups and started the process. He and Nick obviously knew each other pretty well. There'd been no hesitation or anything. No writhing small talk.

"Still milk and two?"

"Thanks, Steve, yeah. I won't be long."

Steve looked through a magazine while the water boiled. It had black and white photos of jazz musicians on duty.

"You wait till you hear Nick play... Nick! have you got anything this week?"

"Gigs? No, there's something of a drought."

"In Sydney? Don't gimme that."

"It's true. Hold on, I'll be out in a minute."

The whistle blew, and Steve made the coffee. Nick emerged putting his tie on. His hair was slicked straight back. His shirt was white. His pants weren't flared. This was unusual behaviour for the time, even among bank employees. It was almost like a parody of conservatism. It took nerve. I was impressed.

"Let me explain, Steve. There's a drought for *me*, because I don't chase the work. You know my situation. I'm not broke, and I get the same kick whether I play for a thousand people or — "

"A stray cat."

"Exactly. I'm an amateur in the true sense. But you know all that. How was your trip? Did you drive through the night?"

"No, we slept in the bus. You were in darkness, we didn't want to knock."

"You should have. Never mind, you're here now... Don't tell me. Abe Lincoln. You're growing slack, Steve. Where's the rest of the costume?"

"Hey! Leave me alone. Anyway, it's not Lincoln. We're joining the land rush. I told you on the phone."

"Ah yes. The exodus. Stephanus Agricola. Why don't you just play music, and forget all these sub-plots?"

"Why don't *you* just play music, and forget — "

"Yes, of course. Touché. Wanda. You write songs, I'm told."

"Lyrics, yeah."

"And do you have a working partner, a composer? Steve's not very expansive on the phone, as you're doubtless aware."

"There's a guy in America, Lloyd Moss. Do you know Clearspots?"

"Clearspots? Yes, I do. I bought *Flagging Down Chance* at an import shop."

"Well, some of those songs are mine. The title track and three others."

"Wonderful! I take my hat off. Steve tells me nothing. And Clearspots are recording a second album, I hear."

"Yep. It's due out mid-year."

"Some of your lyrics?"

"Thirteen songs."

"Is that the whole album?"

"Yep."

Nick gave a whistle of approval and suddenly glanced anxiously at the clock. Steve laughed.

"What's the hurry? It's not even eight o'clock."

"I always walk."

"Skip it, I'll drive you."

"No, no. If I change my routine, anything could happen. We'll chat more tonight. Six twenty three I get back. Approximately. Ha! Ha!"

"Yeah, I know. If you're aware of your mania, you're not crazy."

"You're the expert, Steve. See you both tonight. Here's a spare key. Treat this as your home. I really must go."

He dashed out. Steve was still laughing.

"That guy accounts for every second of his life. We've probably wrecked his day already. He'll have to run... You got the nod, Wanda. It counts, too. Nick can be a vicious critic." Steve returned to the magazine.

Again he'd been teasing me with hints. He must have known Nick would be forthright about the Phases. It was obviously a time-honoured game between them. He'd probably even guessed his friend would say 'Lincoln'. It was all pretty strange, but I wouldn't bite. Steve would have to look me in the eye and say, "Okay, Wanda, I'm a department store dummy." Otherwise I'd stick to my own script, my raw prawn stance. Plays within plays weren't enough. It had to be all or nothing. I was in no hurry. Besides, there was important work to be done — the Simon Question. I wasn't about to let *that* slip, just because of the staggering odds.

"Shall we go to The Rocks today?"

"... To look for your mate? Yeah, if you like."

"Do you know how to get there?"

"It's near the Bridge. It'll have to be the public bus, we'd never get a park."

"Okay. You can be the guide until I piece it all together."

"You won't do that in three days."

"No, I guess not."

There were lots of passengers. We must have caught the tag of peak hour. We had to stand up. I felt a bit crook.

"We should eat soon, Steve. What did we have yesterday? Bliss Bars and fizzwater."

177

"And hippie biscuits."

"Ah, that's right. Better than nothing."

"I should have grabbed that velvet thing, Wanda. That wizard suit the guy left."

What was this? More tomfoolery? Another glimpse behind the curtain? It was getting tedious. I wasn't buying. 'All or Nothing,' I reminded myself, and didn't reply. Steve didn't persist. If he ended up winning this absurd tussle, it would at least be a split decision. I refused to lie down. The rest of the journey passed in silence. That didn't bother me. There was plenty to see. In the city we grabbed a snack. At Circular Quay it was. Free entertainment. I could have hung around there all day, watching the ferries, gazing at the Bridge, the new Opera House, the crush of speedy citizens. But we had a task, a delicate commission. We'd have to go through the motions at least.

Checking the street book first would have been smart. We'd forgotten. We strolled down to the general area and enquired. It didn't take long to find the building. A child could have done that. Now the hard part, the cagey landlord, primed and bribed. We knocked and waited. There wasn't a peep, and we repeated the dose. A shuffle this time. The door opened, and a purple face checked us out. The guy had a moth-eaten singlet stretched over his beer belly.

"Yeah?"

"Are you the landlord?"

"Nah, this one's in the wife's name. Most of my buildings are on the north side." Gallows humour. Fair enough. I'd asked for it.

"Is he here?"

"Who wants to know, sister?"

"I'm really looking for someone else..." I gave him Simon's alias.

"Haven't seen 'im for a couple of weeks."

"A couple of weeks? You know him then?"

"I know who ya mean. We all mind our own business."

"But does he still live here?"

"Wouldn't know. Is that all?"

"Could I see the landlord?"

"Try the office. Tell 'im the front door was open."

He disappeared through one of the battered doors. Steve and I crept down the corridor. At the far end, there was a rough partition with a radio scratching quietly behind it. I coughed. A guy stuck his head over the top.

"Was that door open again? Whadda ya want?"

I knew it was futile, but I gave him the name.

"Never 'eard of 'im."

Steve was trying to look tough, but it hadn't made any difference.

"Could I just leave a note? It's important. I know he'll want to see me."

"Well, you'd better find out where 'e lives then."

I was no Gilbert. I didn't have a clue how to bust this kind of wall. We headed back towards the street door. I stopped at the first guy's room, and scribbled out a note for Simon.

"What's Nick's phone number?"

Steve dug out his address book. I knocked. We got the shuffle and the face.

"What now?"

"Is twenty bucks any good to you?"

"If yer gonna throw it away."

"Here you are. And give this note to my friend."

"Dunno if I'll see 'im."

"Well, if you do."

"It's no skin off my nose."

I'd made a clumsy move. Open-ended. Wasteful. I knew all that, but it was my only chance. Steve and I left. I had no sense of accomplishment. If anything I felt like I'd been mugged. But at least I'd be able to report a recent sighting to Mr Mordecai. Unless the guy had made it up. It would have been a moronic lie, of course. He hadn't expected money at that point. But people aren't always driven by reason. I'd noticed *that* a couple of times. Anyway, that was that, for the moment. I'd try and shake off my gloom. This was Sydney, after all. The water sparkled.

"Steve, let's go on a ferry."

"Where to?"

"Anywhere. Just a cruise."

"Manly Beach? That's over on the other side."

"Okay."

We stood on the deck. There wasn't much of a crowd. Sydney people are spoilt I guess. The harbour's no adventure for them. It's just a short cut to and fro. I even saw a few passengers reading newspapers.

I wondered what I'd do if I ever got like that. Blasé, tired, unappreciative. I couldn't look at them any more. I turned to the water. On every side, buildings seemed to perch on its edge. Citizens fighting over the view. Why wouldn't they? Few prizes glittered like *this* one. Again I had the idea that you'd have to be crazy not to live here. I wished we could just look for a room straight away, and not bother about anything else. It even occurred to me to do exactly that, and let Steve go north on his own. It didn't seem like cricket though. And four weeks in the bush wouldn't hurt. In fact, it might even sharpen my appetite for this harbour and this town...

Steve leaned on the rail a few feet away. He was smoking a small cigar. A rare thing. Even more unusual than his wearing denim. A cigar meant 'Very deep thought indeed'. I left him to it. I knew I might have to get a job soon. Even if the new album turned out to be huge, I wouldn't see a cracker till the end of the year. Another small advance maybe, if I asked. I remembered an amusing formula that Lloyd had mentioned in a letter. The Clearspots' motto it was. BT^2B. It stood for 'Bigger Than The Beatles'. That would be handy. I didn't get carried away though. I knew a bit about probability. Just the same, if the first album was any indication I'd find myself in a cushy spot in a few months' time. Cushy for me, anyway. My demands were still pretty modest I think.

I'd have to write a couple of letters. Manly Beach would do for that, if I could find a sheltered spot. I'd send a note to Mr Mordecai outlining the unwieldy steps I'd taken. And the alleged sighting of course, without laying too much emphasis on its validity. I'd write to Mum and Dad as well. They'd be pleased to hear from me. Also, Lloyd had their address as a contact. I'd take the liberty of using Nick's place for my Sydney poste restante...

On the north side of the harbour, there was a vast patch of scrub, a national park presumably. I wondered how long you'd last if you tried camping in there. It would certainly amount to a bob each way. You could scribble songs amid the bird calls, riding at the same time on urban tension's lusty wings. I'd think about it.

"Impressive, yes?"

"Steve, let's decide *now.*"

"You know we can't. What about Morris?"

"Why don't you contact him? He may have had second thoughts or something."

"I doubt it. The world doesn't change key because someone happens to like Sydney."

"Yeah, I know. But make sure. We don't want to drive up there for nothing. I thought I might post off a letter or two from Manly. You could do the same. Write to Morris and give him Nick's number. Or better still, send a telegram."

"Okay, okay."

Steve could easily have reassured me. He could have said we'd be back in a month whatever happened. But he didn't. There was obviously other stuff going on. He was Thinking. I'd have to wait.

We bounded down the plank. We got ice-cream and sauntered here and there. That's what you did at Manly. No one seemed to be in much of a hurry. I bought paper and envelopes, and we found a coffee shop. I scrawled out my messages, and we got more ice-cream. At the post office, Steve telegraphed his brother. "Confirm instructions." That's all it said. Steve decided to find a cheap watch. He did that, and we had a couple of beers. We'd hardly ever sat in a bar for no particular reason. I guess we were at a loose end. After a while, Steve spread out the timetable he'd picked up at Circular Quay. He checked his wrist with a frown. Just like a kid.

"We've got...fourteen minutes, Wanda. One for the road?"

We spent two or three hours looking around the city, lounging in Hyde Park, stuff like that. Apart from the distraction of his watch, Steve didn't seem all that excited about anything. He was cheerful enough I guess, but pretty quiet. Those early beers had perhaps slowed him down a bit. By about four, I was starting to get drowsy myself. We decided to catch a taxi back to Bondi.

Steve kept glancing at his new toy. It seemed like every couple of minutes. It probably wasn't that often. I wondered briefly whether he was going to slip into a Nick-style obsession with time, but it didn't really seem likely. It wasn't specific enough from a dramatic point of view. There was no uniform, no definitive mode of speech. Anyone could do it.

Back at the house, we sprawled out on the living room floor and looked at magazines. We soon dozed. Nick's return woke us. Steve consulted his wrist immediately.

"Yes! Six twenty-three. A gold star."

"Hi Steve, hi Wanda."

Nick put down his briefcase and went to the kitchen. He came back in loosening his tie.

"How was your day?"

"Steve and I went to Manly for a while, and hung around in town."

"Sounds like fun. How do you have your coffee?"

"Both black, no sugar. Thanks."

"That's easy enough. Excuse me, I'll just go and change. Put a record on if you like."

Steve didn't get up, but I had a casual glance at some of the titles. It was a pretty healthy collection. Mostly jazz, as I'd assumed, but several boxes of other music too, all of them carefully labelled. Classical was divided into symphonies, piano concerti, violin concerti, and so on. Rock was alphabetical. And there was a Miscellaneous section, consisting of Blues, Ragtime, Folk and Other. I checked Other. I figured a sub-category of Miscellaneous would be worth a look. Nick came in with the coffee. He'd put on grey trousers, and a pale yellow cardigan. And slip-on shoes.

"Found anything? Play your Clearspots if you like. But I suppose you've heard it far too often already."

"Not that often. Maybe ten times."

"Only ten times?"

"Yeah, about that. I checked out the copy Lloyd sent me. Played it for a few people. Gave it to my parents. I'd rather start something new than swim in the old stuff."

"How strange... So you don't collect records?"

"No, no. I don't collect anything. Memories, I guess, if you want to put it that way. But even there, I'm not particularly nostalgic."

"How strange. But you must appreciate music?"

"Ha! Of course. I'll listen to any piece once. But that's usually enough, even if I really like it."

"... Most extraordinary. What about Aboriginal music?"

"It's okay. I haven't listened to much. There was a guy in Melbourne I heard a couple of times. In Fitzroy. He dared to play in the street. The cops didn't like it, you can imagine."

"Yes. Yes. Unfortunately I can. Was he a friend of yours?"

"Nah, not really. I approached him once, but he wasn't very sociable. He'd had enough of people generally, I think."

"Yes. Yes, I suppose it happens. I've got something on tape. You can give me your thoughts."

Nick uncovered a reel-to-reel machine, and loaded it. He checked his detailed notes, and sped the tape forward to the correct spot. The guy was organized.

"Right. Here we are. Steve! Didgeridoo music. Do you want to hear it? Looks like he's out for the count. Never mind."

The tape started turning. A faint drone at first. A bit like an OM, in some ways. The volume gradually increased, but there was no other change. The sound just hung there. Pitch and tone were constant. After a couple of minutes, the volume levelled out too. It worked like a chant. If you got into it, nothing else moved or mattered. I got into it.

Suddenly there was a loud GWAH! Steve jumped up with his mouth open. He didn't talk. He just knelt there staring at space. That's pretty much what *I* was doing.

The music took off at an angle. All sorts of choppy stuff crept in. There was no other instrument. Whatever was happening came from tonal changes alone. It was a class act. I felt like a mug, hearing it first from a white guy. Nick must have thought I was a complete clown. I chucked out these distracting notions. I was present at something special. The catalyst didn't matter.

The music finally descended through another drone, and slipped away somewhere. No one talked for ages. Eventually, Nick broke the silence. He looked across at me and Steve.

"Yes?" That's all he said.

We just nodded. The situation wasn't embarrassing. Just kind of holy or something...

"This is new to you, Wanda?"

I had to own up. Nick must have already seen my astonishment. The guy I'd heard in Melbourne hadn't sounded like *this*.

"It's new to me, yes. I'd rather not comment on it, Nick."

"That's alright… Unfortunately, I don't know the musician's name. A friend of mine made the recording last year, in Western Australia. It interests me greatly. From the technical side as much as anything."

"You mean you're trying it yourself?"

"Not exactly, Steve. Not the didgeridoo. But you can imagine the musical doors that circular breathing opens… I'm working on its perfection. You can't just pick it up like a riff."

"I guess not. Who did the recording? Someone I know?"

"I don't think so. His name's Bill Jacob. 'Jake the Snake' he prefers. He's started up a theatre group over in Newtown. Mainly for his own people, but they've got two or three white kids as well. He's the guy who's clueing me up on the endless breath technique."

"So this Jake's a player too?"

"Yes, he's a player. Nothing like what we just heard, as he'd readily admit, but he can do it up to a point. Certainly enough to give me a few tips. We can go and see him if you like. Saturday, perhaps. You'll still be here, won't you?"

"Yeah, yeah. Till Sunday morning at least. What do you think, Wanda?"

"A visit? Of course."

"Alright, people, I'll set it up. Now, as for tonight's program, we could go out and eat. Or see a band. You decide. Oh, Steve, I should have thought of it this morning.

You can park the bus in the street round the back. I wouldn't leave it unattended on the esplanade. Not overnight."

"Okay, I'll get onto it later. Do you want to go out, Wanda?"

"I wouldn't mind."

"Well, I need a shower. You two discuss it."

Nick put the kettle on again. I wasn't sure I wanted to hear a band, but a restaurant might be okay. I'd wait and see what Nick suggested. He wouldn't come up with anything raucous. I could count on that.

"Ah! Milk! I'm out of step today, Wanda. I'll dash down to the corner. Six minutes."

He vanished. The kettle boiled and I turned it off. It was nowhere near six minutes yet. The phone rang. There were clicks and squeaks at first, then some action.

"Is Steve there? I'm calling from Adelaide! Oh, is that Wanda? It's Morris. You guys must be psychic. I've been tearing my hair out. Everything's gone ape. They've all backed out. They formed a committee, and agreed to lose their nerve! I didn't know how to reach — Hullo! No, it's okay, I'm feeding coins in! Is Steve there?"

"He's in the shower, Morris. I'll see if — "

"No, no. It's okay. It's bets off, that's all. I just wanted — Hullo! Yeah, I was telling Jill I didn't know where you — "

Another click. This one counted. There was only a purring noise now. I felt an odd rush. I'd analyse it later maybe. I went into the bathroom.

"Steve!"

"Guess what. I forgot about the watch. Can you see if it's still ticking? There on the bench."

"Steve, I just had a call from Morris."

He stuck his head out. "What did he say?"

"The deal's off. Everyone's chickened out."

Steve turned off the shower and grabbed a towel. "So he's abandoned the whole idea?"

"I guess so. For now, anyway. *Our* bit's finished."

"Is he angry?"

"Well, he's not too pleased. He was relieved to reach us though. Hm! He thinks we're psychic."

"Well, it *was* a good idea, the telegram. Did you know this would happen?"

"Of course not. I just thought it would be worth a buck to make sure — Hang on, Nick's back from the shop. I'd better tell him what's happening."

"Okay. I'll be out in a minute."

Steve had seemed unmoved. I don't know what I'd expected from him. Relief? Disappointment for Morris? Disappointment for himself? Hard to say. And what did this new situation amount to, anyway? It meant we'd have to reach a decision, and act on it, in the next couple of days. We couldn't disrupt Nick's life any longer than that. Was I excited? Uneasy? I didn't know yet.

"Nick."

"Yes, Wanda."

"Steve's brother rang. Our project's on hold."

"Why? What happened?"

"Oh, Morris had backers, and now he hasn't. That's all."

"Are you upset?"

"Not particularly. Not at all, in fact. I want to live in Sydney. I'd never seen it till yesterday. You must know how it gets you."

"It's my home town, Wanda, but yes, I know how it gets you. What about Steve? He's never spent more than three months on the trot here, if I recall."

"Did I hear a 'What about Steve?' Look at this, Nick. I've only had it since lunchtime." Steve shook the two-bob watch and held it to his ear.

"Big changes, Drum-major? What now?"

Nick didn't muck around. He didn't bother to humour Steve. I should have adopted that sort of tone right from the start.

"Well, Niccolo, these things happen."

"They do, and have, Stephanus. But what's your reaction? This is what vox populi is asking."

"Right now, I'll re-park the bus. Unless we're driving somewhere. What's been decided?"

"Very little, it seems. Here's your coffee. Come on, we'll talk in the living room."

"You drink mine, Wanda. I'll move the bus. I need to think."

Steve rattled his keys and left. Nick and I went to the living room and sat down.

"Dare we listen to more music, Wanda? Is it too soon after the desert song?"

"No, that's okay. You decide."

Nick found something peaceful, and played it quietly. Solo piano it was. Debussy I think. I didn't care anyway... Steve was capable of lurching off into the night for good. It wouldn't have surprised me. I wasn't about to say anything to Nick. He'd probably guessed my thoughts anyway. He'd certainly known Steve long enough to realize he might not see him for another two years. Or twenty.

We sat there without talking for about twenty minutes. One side of the record anyway, whatever that was. Nick flipped it over and we did the same thing again. He shut his eyes this time, that was the only difference. Side two finished, and he stood up.

"I'm going to cook something, Wanda. Perhaps an omelette. Are you hungry?"

"No. No thanks, Nick."

"Play any music you want."

"Okay. Thanks."

He went off to the kitchen. I didn't bother with the records, I tried to focus on my plans. I knew I'd stay in Sydney for sure whatever Steve did. I thought about my work, Lloyd's forthcoming album, the scraps of new songs I'd been playing with... I must admit, everything looked a bit gloomy. Suddenly I heard the back door open.

"This town's got more cars than people, Nick. Where's your miraculous parking spot? I drove up here, then back to the beach, and lost the one I had. I found somewhere at Neutral Bay."

"You're kidding!"

"Of course. But I'm a mile away at least."

"C'est la vie. Do you want food?"

"Yeah, I wouldn't mind."

"Sure you're not hungry, Wanda? It's not too late to say!"

I strolled into the kitchen. "Well, yeah, I might have something. Thanks, Nick."

Despite this reprieve, the next day was pretty flat. Steve and I hung around Bondi Beach, looking at the ocean and the people. There wasn't much left of summer. General melancholy had its foot in the door. It was a bit windy. Newspapers flew around. Seagulls huddled. We sat in a couple of coffee shops. We skipped the pubs. Steve bought another watch, water-resistant supposedly.

Nick had phoned Jake the Snake. On Saturday afternoon we hopped in a cab for Newtown. Steve's bus wouldn't have been suitable for the inner city. We'd have driven around for ever, like The Flying Dutchman. I'm not sure what I'd expected, but Jake's theatre was just a house. Not even a big house. The front door was closed, but apparently not locked — there was a note pinned to it. 'Please Enter Quietly'. We crept down the hall, Nick in the lead. At the end was a thick curtain. We slipped through, and stood still.

The daylight had been shut out. A couple of red spots were aimed at the far end of the room. Three young black guys were on the floor, in a kind of push-up position. Completely still, though. Music came from a speaker a few feet to our left. It was didgeridoo, plus something percussive...

The spotlights were then replaced by yellow ones. It had seemed instantaneous, but the people on the stage now held slightly different poses. I hadn't seen them move. Next time I'd be ready, and watch more carefully. But there wasn't a next time. They stayed put, and a new dancer appeared among them. A bloke of average height but exceptionally thin.

"Jake the Snake," whispered Nick.

Jake rippled and writhed, and formed spectacular angles with his arms and neck, none of the positions lasting more than a second or two. The music had built up, and it now finished with a loud GWAH! I was familiar with the GWAH! but that's about all I knew. I suddenly felt a bit uneasy about meeting Jake. The spotlights had vanished with the music. Now someone switched on an overhead light.

The three guys on the stage were standing up, and Jake was addressing them quietly, with an occasional gesture. There were five other people sitting on the floor. Two black girls, a white girl, and two white guys, all in their late teens, I'd say. I wasn't sure if they knew we were there. Anyway, they didn't show it. They whispered together. About the performance, it seemed. One of them kept pointing to the stage. Jake happened to see Nick, and nodded, but he didn't come over. The five on the floor turned to glance at us, but that was all. They got straight back to their discussion. It was clearly a serious business.

Eventually, Jake sent the dancers off, and signalled to the other five. They stood up, and collected chairs from behind a side curtain. They placed them in a half-circle on the stage, and Jake walked off, with a glance towards the opposite end of the room. Someone hidden up there got rid of the overhead light, and trained a white beam onto the performance area. The five sat cross-legged on the chairs. A dialogue began between the black girls, then they froze, and a three-way chat sprung up among the whites... Various combinations followed in this manner, weaving a tight word-play of about ten minutes' duration. It was sharp stuff alright, a quick-change act, and no slips. The spot went off, the overhead on.

"Twenty minutes!" Jake called. Then he came over to see us.

"Nick."

They shook hands, and Steve and I were introduced.

Jake looked older close up. He could have been forty. Athletic though, as I've pointed out. Nick praised what we'd seen, but Jake laughed.

"A sketch. Come back when it's been sandpapered. We'll eventually have two hours of precision, if the children are up to it."

He indicated the cast. The lights guy had joined them. They were all smoking, and talking, and mucking around. It was true that they didn't look much when the pressure was off. Jake and Nick chatted easily. The subject of my lucky knack with words arose, and Jake pounced. He glared straight into my eyes. The name 'Jake the Snake' referred to more than his slim build.

"You can write for our theatre." It wasn't a question.

"Three-minute songs, Jake. That's all I can do."

"You mean it's all you've done so far."

"Well, yes."

He spoke to Steve. "You are obviously a performer. What do you do?"

"Some say I'm a drummer."

"And what do you say?"

"Okay. I'm a drummer."

"Come this way, all of you."

Jake led us back up the hall, and into a bedroom. He handed out wooden blocks to Steve and Nick. Then he sat down at an upright piano, and established a rhythm based on one chord. The tapping blocks backed him up.

"Good. We have ten minutes. We'll use it profitably. Wanda, please recite two of your songs in succession."

It wasn't a suitable time to argue. I went along with it. Overall, it didn't sound bad, except that the seam showed.

"Good. That's enough, Wanda. For someone who can

write these lyrics, constructing a graceful chain is a simple exercise. Thank you, Nick, Steve. We'll go back."

We went back. Jake clapped his hands.

"In two minutes, children, you will be prepared."

Cigarettes were put out, and talk became intermittent.

"Nick. You arrived at the time I said, as always. Thank you. You saw what you were supposed to see. For the next part of our proceeding, I'll have to insist on privacy. None of you will have any trouble understanding this, I'm sure." Jake ushered us up the hall again, and took the note off the door. "Thank you all again. Wanda, Nick has my telephone number. I'll see you presently. Farewell."

He closed the door. We heard the latch click. Steve wasn't pleased.

"A waste of time, Nick."

"I'm not so sure about that."

"Who does that guy think he is?"

"I wouldn't know, but I'll give you my *own* view. He's man with plenty of work to do, and none of it easy. He ca dispense with needless distraction."

"There was no reason to kick us out. We were qui enough."

"For God's sake, Steve, it was a rehearsal. He didr have to invite us at all. You know how these things are. W headed up to the main road. King Street, it was called. W hung around, and looked in shop windows. We play(tourists. I'd made no snap decision on Jake's proposal, b any vague doubts about living in Sydney had certain gone. I wasn't likely to abscond.

At about five, we went to a Lebanese restaurant. I didr talk much. Steve and Nick discussed various jazz playe1 comparing some of the Johnny-come-latelies with O

Masters. Their chat grew fiery now and then. The food was great, and there was no sense of being hustled along. Nick mentioned some young piano hot-shot, a local guy. He'd be performing later in the night, somewhere in King's Cross. We thought we might go up there and have a listen. After a couple of hours and a few drinks, we got a cab into the city and saw a Swedish film. It was okay I guess. Something about a desperate knight and his loud side-kick. I wasn't really in the mood. After that, we checked out the piano bloke, and agreed on his importance.

Sunday morning wasn't exactly a deadline, but it was time to consider getting out of Nick's hair. Not that he'd deviated from Perfect Gent. Certainly not. The three of us were sitting in his backyard. It was just warm enough, in the sunny part. We had lemon tea and toast with raisins in it. Nick spoke up.

"So. You'll both be applying for citizenship, I take it. We'll be neighbours."

"Not a bad idea. What do you think, Steve?"

"I'm going to sea."

"Why not decide now?"

"I'm going to sea, Wanda. S.E.A. Shiver me timbers."

Nick dropped his toast. I jumped up shouting.

"Steve! Are you crazy? What are you talking about?"

"I'm going to Mallacoota. Abalone diving."

Nick looked on in horror. I didn't feel so great either. What had happened to the once peerless diplomat?

"Steve! Is this a gag, or what?"

"No. A friend has a boat there. He asked me last time I was here in Sydney. I suddenly remembered it the other night, when we parked at the beach."

"Last time you were here? How long's that? Four years or something! Offers don't just float in the air forever!'

"He's always hiring deckhands. And even if he's not, he'll make room for me. It's big business, Wanda."

Nick had withdrawn quietly into the house. I was furious.

"So what will you wear?" I snarled at Steve.

"Bring me a knife."

"What for?"

"Bring it and you'll see."

I went inside.

"Nick! Oh, there you are." I lowered my voice. "Steve wants a knife. He's cracking up I think."

"A knife? What for?"

"Who knows? He's mad."

Nick went to a drawer and selected a fierce looking thing. A steak knife I think.

"You're not giving him *that*?"

"I've never known Steve to be violent. At least, not murderously so. Besides, I'm familiar with self-defence techniques. You stay here at the door."

Nick went out and put the potential weapon on the table. Steve picked it up quietly, and stuck the point in his jeans, just above the knee. He hacked through the material and ripped the trouser leg off. Same again on the other leg. Then he took one of the discarded pieces and cut off a strip. This he tied round his head. He wasn't laughing. He stood up.

"Like I said. Shiver me timbers."

He gripped the knife in his teeth for a second, and then handed it back to Nick. He walked straight past me into the house. Nick just stood there. I was a bit vague too. I

196

heard Steve scuffling around inside. Then he left by the front door. I sat down on the kitchen steps. I wondered if our tea was still hot.

* * *

There was no harbour view. My room was in Newtown. Not because of Jake's theatre. When I'd moved, I was still deciding on that. I happened to like Newtown, that's all. And it was cheap. Cheap for Sydney, anyway. I spent the first few days loitering in King Street, distracting myself with the constant parade. After a week or so of this, I phoned Jake. I guess I'd known from the start that I would, but I had to be sure of myself. There'd be no backing out. You don't sabotage that level of dedication.

"Bill Jacob."

"Hullo Jake, it's Wanda."

"Yes. How's eight o'clock tonight, for a discussion?"

"At your place?"

"In the theatre, yes."

"Okay, I'll be there. Should I bring anything?"

"Thoughts. As many as possible."

"Okay, see you then."

"Good."

This guy didn't muck around. I knew we'd get on. I went straight back to my room, and glanced through my notes. My outlines, my beginnings and ends, and hooks. Most of the stuff was geared to the radio ditty formula. But I also had scraps of poems, and summaries of ideas. These I gathered up. I figured our first talk would deal mainly with general aims and so on, but I thought I should be ready for specifics. I stuck my papers in a shoulder-bag and took off again. So far, I'd used my room only for sleeping. Soon it would be an office as well.

I had a couple of hours to fill in. I decided to walk randomly for a while, and then start circling back. I'd bought my own two-bob watch — it would have to be my last luxury for the moment. I'd probably need to bite Lloyd at some stage, for another advance. He'd still be in San Francisco, tampering with the album. If it happened to be a commercial dog, I'd owe him, that's all. I'd wash dishes. I was too busy to look for a job straight away. Besides, I wasn't completely broke. I still had a bit left from my last cheque, despite a few careless moments. It wasn't much though. Enough for two months perhaps, if I gave up buying coffee.

As I walked, I steered my thoughts away from bread and butter and tried to anticipate Jake's questions. I tried to form a picture of his game plan, before I even knew the full scope of his ambition. Not easy. And pointless anyway. I'd know soon enough. Naturally, Steve's image leapt into my meditations again and again. I didn't offer him a chair.

It seemed strange that I hadn't taken a shot at more difficult projects before. Maybe I'd grown slack from getting lucky so early in the piece. Writing songs was certainly a satisfying thing in its way, and I couldn't bitch about the wages either. I wondered how long Clearspots would thrive. That probably wasn't the right word anyway. They weren't chauffeur-driven, or any of that stuff. They were a cult. But an American cult. Meaning they could eat without having to wash cars. 'Cult' had different connotations in Australia. Well-dressed martyrdom was the most it could aspire to. I wondered if this would ever change.

I got to my appointment on the dot.

"Wanda. Please come in. Coffee or tea?"

"Black coffee thanks, no sugar."

"I'll see to it. That's your seat."

Jake had led me to his theatre room. Most of it was in darkness. A spotlight was rigged up over a trestle-table. There were two chairs, one on either side. I sat down and waited. After a couple of minutes, Jake reappeared with the coffee. Someone followed him, a kid about sixteen. I recognized him as the lights operator.

"Wanda, this is my son, Ray."

"Hi, Ray."

"Hi, Wanda."

"Homework now. You can talk to Wanda another time."

Ray bounded away. Jake sat down and addressed me.

"Right. Here are my cards, face up. At this time in Australia our race counts for nothing. As a group, that is. But a few individuals have refused to accept the slamming doors. I am one. Unless my perception is sliding, you are another. My son, and the young performers of my troupe, are further examples. Forget the white members for the moment, I'll come to that presently. The aim of this company is to produce theatre of incontestable excellence. I want people's eyes to hurt because they've forgotten to blink. I want to enter the foyer after a performance and hear nothing from the milling throng except its breathing. Unless, of course, there are journalists in attendance — I don't expect miracles, Wanda. I am a realist. People are what they are...

"This brings me to my next point. Only the best are admitted to our circle. No one is invited just for being black, and no one is turned away for reasons of whiteness. The best are in. The others can wait. I've been criticized for this attitude, but I won't bend. The moment I allow mediocrity, I become known as a director of novelties, of cuteness. White people who don't loathe our race often see us as children. They'll applaud any fumbling attempt on our part. They'll patronize us. Personally I'd rather dodge apple cores. My company will dazzle, or it will not perform.

"At the moment, I am the sole writer and choreographer. Not because I insist on being a despot, but because none of the others is *yet* capable of contributing in either of these areas. They are only in their teens, after all. This structure will change if you join us. I'm offering you a six week trial. I can't promise you money at present. We're called Day One Productions. Are you interested?"

"Yes, I'm interested. Assuming that you *can* reduce the audience to a stunned silence, where do you think your work will lead?"

"It will lead to our race being treated as human beings. Apparently, a publicly demonstrated capacity for excellence is essential for this. Otherwise, the current situation will persist, a situation in which the most we can expect is a pat on the head from well-meaning groups who'd do the same for a dog, if its ear happened to flop at the correct angle — the cute child syndrome that I touched on earlier."

"And theatre is the only means of sorting these things out?"

"Not the only means, but the quickest. Except perhaps for television, but I can't see much happening in that quarter until the ball is already rolling. It's up to us."

200

"Okay, I'm in."

"Good. Here's the program. I want to put on three shows in the last week of July. I've already booked the premises, and paid. There can't be any refund. Just the same, if the standard isn't reached, I won't hesitate to cancel. I want two hours of flawless performance. So far, we have about forty minutes that's somewhere near the mark. An additional forty minutes exists on paper. This part is in the very early stages of rehearsal. So early, that I'm not yet sure whether it will work as I want it to. The other third is yours. I'd like a first draft from you in four weeks. Can you handle it?"

"I'll soon find out, Jake."

"If you can't, I'll be genuinely astounded. I'll have to rethink my life. Hah! Don't let me frighten you."

"...But what if I hadn't shown up? You must have already had a plan."

"Well, I suppose I would have settled for a ninety minute show, or thereabouts. I hadn't admitted this to anyone. First I would have tried to complete the quota myself — very difficult, because of my other work. Stores clerk. I won't go into it...We rehearse in three hour blocks. Eight p.m. Monday, Wednesday, Thursday. Saturday, two till five. No one is late. The prima donna stance is unknown around my theatre. Hah! Except in the level of achievement, of course. I'll give you copies of the existing scripts, to help you with continuity. Just a guide. There'll be three distinct sections. Yours is yours. Secrecy is crucial. Any questions?"

"When should I come back?"

"Why not tomorrow night's rehearsal? Witness the whole thing, meet the other culprits."

"Okay."

Jake stood up and led me into the hall. He got the script from his bedroom, and wrote down my address.

"Thank you, Wanda. I'm sorry to have to rush you, but I must torment my notes. They're never quite right. Hardly ever. It's the same with songs, no doubt."

"Yeah, it is a bit like that. I'll see you tomorrow, Jake."

When I got back to my room, I boiled the dregs from the coffee jar and sprawled out to look over Jake's work. Much of it was ballet talk, notes on various sequences. This stuff meant nothing to me. It was technical, and it was detailed, and no doubt it was spot on, but the language wasn't mine. It wouldn't reach me until I saw it happening on stage.

These sections I plucked out, leaving a mass of dialogue, and more general directions. I soon realized Jake was a master. He could juggle words any way he liked. He could chuck them around at random, and force them to land in a straight line, or a circle, or a star shape. It was all the same to him. He could force them to hang in the air for a second or two, if he needed the time for something else. He could talk them into rhyming, he could bounce them off another character's remarks, or draw them out in counterpoint and catch them in his hat. It was intimidating in a way. I was glad I hadn't signed anything.

The next morning, I went through it again. The script was no less impressive as a whole, but this time I analysed individual parts over and over. And I studied the way they were tied together. My nerve picked up. Eventually I was convinced that I could in fact 'construct a graceful chain', as Jake had suggested at our first meeting. I'd stick to my guns of course. There'd be no point in trying to imitate the style of the existing work. My stuff wouldn't even be vaguely similar. Nor should it be. But I knew there was no cause for alarm. In four weeks, I'd be able to churn out a vibrant contribution for sure. No problem.

Most of that night's rehearsal was slow and disjointed. Nothing like the few minutes I'd seen a week or so previously. Jake kept putting the brakes on. He strode around fiddling with the smallest details. But when the cast finally went through it in one hit, he was satisfied.

"Yes! Most certainly!" he shouted. His adjustments had paid off.

The kids left, except for Ray of course, who went off to bed. Jake saw my new confidence. I didn't have to spell anything out. We talked again. It was easier this time. No spotlight, no sense of interview. We just talked. I got a better idea of the commercial side of the situation. The place he'd booked for the public performance was nothing swish. It wasn't large either. It could hold about one hundred people. Jake would be content if he pulled in two hundred over the three nights. This seemed pretty modest to me, considering the time spent on rehearsals, and the high standard that would prevail. I mentioned these things.

"Wanda. We're not the Bolshoi. We're not the London Philharmonic. There won't be any ticket scalpers. Not yet. It's 1972. In 1982, we'll see. In '92... Well, it's anyone's guess. Our troupe will no longer exist, of course. But Aboriginal theatre will mean something — as long as the level of peformance is beyond question. That's the only aspect under *my* jurisdiction, and I'll get it right, Wanda."

I wasn't about to argue. We drifted on to other topics. I left around eleven thirty. Jake had to get up early for work.

203

The following Saturday, Nick dropped in to deliver a thank-you card from Mr Mordecai. Also a short letter from Mum. I wrote to Lloyd for money...

I'd started on my script, but it was still more or less shapeless. I plugged away at it for another week or so, and called in to read Jake my synopsis. He seemed pleased enough. I didn't see him again for a fortnight. Then I presented the finished work. I was three days inside the first draft deadline. I didn't stick around.

We met again on the Tuesday to discuss my submission. Again he approved. In fact, he said he wouldn't need another draft. There was enough for him to build on. As director, he was of course free to make changes. I left it with him, saying I'd come round now and again to watch a rehearsal. There'd been no response from Simon, of course. I'd asked Nick to send me a telegram if he got a call. It was nearly six weeks since I'd left my note at The Rocks. There was nothing more I could do. I was getting into my songs again. Some of them were falling into place easily, others resisted arrest. The usual story.

No word from Lloyd either. I must admit I felt a bit uneasy. I'd soon be completely penniless. My room was paid up a month ahead, but I wasn't eating much. I sometimes recalled the arrogant tips I'd flung around, like that twenty dollars to Simon's mate, or whoever he was, the purple-faced guy at the rooming house. It was all spilt milk of course. I tried to think of people to ask, if Lloyd didn't come good. Every possibility made me cringe. Eventually, I started toying with the idea of a telegram to America, or even a phone call. International conversation was still a big deal in those days. And you paid in blocks of three minutes. A risky business. In my case, it would amount to gambling with a few days' food.

So what? I decided. All or nothing. I'd get Lloyd's number from information. I'd have to look at the time difference. I didn't want to wake him up in the afternoon. Musicians hate that. I gathered up a bit of cash and went to the post office. It turned out to be night in California. Ten o'clock or something... There was a lot of waiting and mucking around with exchanges, but at last I heard a voice.

"Riffworks! No job too big! Whoozat? Where the hell are ya?"

"Is that Lloyd? I'm calling from Australia. It's Wanda."

"Squander, Lloyd! Squander! Here, grab it!"

"Lloyd Moss speaking. Who's that?"

"Wanda."

"Who?"

"Wanda. Your partner in crime. I'm calling from Sydney. Did you get my letter?"

"Jesus! Shut up, Bob! Wanda! There's no letter..."

"Lloyd, I'm in a mess. Any chance of... you know, a further advance?"

"Hey! Name it! You don't have to beg. This record's a killer! You wait till ya hear the production. We've got — "

"Lloyd! We'll be cut off. Have you got a pen?" I gave him the post office address. I underlined the urgency. I told him five hundred dollars.

"Hey! How about a thousand? We ain't no garage band."

"Thanks Lloyd. I would have been — " Click! Game over...

I went to the Lebanese restaurant.

***

I'd attended the last five rehearsals leading up to opening night. Before that, I'd checked on the progress maybe half a dozen times altogether. Giant steps had been taken. Some of my contribution still came back word for word. Other bits remained only in essence. That was okay. The show ran like clockwork. Jake was ecstatic. He didn't bother to hide it either. The production was to be called *Flying Start*. No tickets had been available in advance. Maybe Jake had considered the danger of a poor response, and didn't want to alarm the cast unnecessarily. Anyway, there'd been plenty of posters, and a few newspaper ads. Everything possible had been done.

With an hour to go, Jake was pacing around backstage. It wasn't nervous pacing. More like some kind of a warm-up. He didn't address the cast at all. He had another job now. Virtuoso dancer. You couldn't do that and call shots as well. Not this late in the day. Anyway, the kids looked relaxed. I guess they had their stuff down alright. It was no school play, no two and a half rehearsals, weather permitting. It was the real McCoy. It was Theatre.

The players and dancers were cued up for their masterpiece. Hair triggers were in place. Jake now sat quietly. In about half an hour, he'd wink or something, and perfection would unfold before the astonished onlookers.

Someone had to check. With twenty minutes left, there should have been murmurs and shuffling. I went up onto the stage, and peeped through the curtains. I counted twenty three people, mostly in pairs, with a few solo punters near the back. Hmm. But there was still plenty of time.

Those present seemed attentive, anyway. Their reaction would count for something. But would it be loud enough?

I felt like a pinhead for considering things in this light, but I was anxious. I was glad I didn't have to appear on stage myself. Even thinking of such an ordeal gave me the shakes. I knew I'd probably never be able to overcome this fear. Publicity equals Horror. That was my formula. Lloyd could have his BT^2B, his Bigger Than The Beatles. It was no good to me.

I climbed down, and walked along the aisle towards the main entrance. I tried to look like Joe Blow, but the assembly stared anyway. They probably mistook me for a star, because of my colour. The customers were all white, except for one guy, a friend of Ray's. I'd met him a couple of times. He was looking at his program, and hadn't noticed me. The ticket-seller was having a smoke. He'd had tougher jobs. In fact he still did. He worked with Jake during the day.

"A bit quiet, Robbo."

"There's still quarter of an hour, Wanda. White folks don't hurry for us. Ha! Ha!" I stuck around there for a while. Another handful of people came in at about five to. I reminded Robbo that no latecomers were to be admitted. Jake's rule. He didn't want the spell broken. I went back in, and took a seat on my own in the last row. I couldn't see Ray. He was crouching up there somewhere among the lighting equipment. His watch had been synchronized with the backstage clock. I focussed on the curtain and waited. Suddenly, there was total darkness. I won't try and paint what followed.

There'd been two short intervals, but I hadn't left my place. At the show's conclusion, there'd been silence at first. Then someone near the front had stood up and applauded. Others soon joined in. There'd been no whistles or shouts, just respectful clapping. No one reappeared on the stage, and after a few minutes the house lights went up. People started to drift out. I guess there'd been a triumph in a way. I wondered what Jake thought. I stayed put for a while after the hall had emptied. Ray had joined his mate, and they'd gone backstage. I waited a bit longer, then headed for the dressing room.

Most of the cast had changed, and were standing around talking. It was hard to nail the general feeling. People relaxing after a job, that was all. Neither high nor low. Jake was sitting alone, with his back to the others. He had his elbows on a table, and his chin on his hands. A couple of feet in front of him, an old travel poster hung on the wall. Naples I think. He probably wouldn't have been looking at that. And he probably wasn't asleep. I got tired of guessing.

"Jake."

He spun around. "Ah, Wanda!" He was beaming. I didn't say anything. He started nodding slowly.

"It worked. It worked. You don't seem pleased, Wanda."

"It worked alright. But the audience…"

"You mean the numbers?" He stood up and put his hands on my shoulders. "Wanda. It's 1972. It worked. Take my word for it."

The other two nights were similar. Flawless performance, small but appreciative crowd. Jake's quiet confidence persisted. Expenses had been covered. There'd be drinks at Newtown.

Jake planned to spend the next few months writing another show. I agreed to contribute. There'd be cast meetings once a week, to keep things intact. Full time

208

rehearsals wouldn't begin until a complete script existed. Probably not till the new year.

That was my first taste of theatre. I'd got the bug alright. Almost straight away, I started wrestling with the next Day One production. My song writing didn't stop either. The release date of Lloyd's album had been changed to the second week of August. I should have guessed there'd be a delay. I still had a bit to learn about Rock'n'roll Time.

**

The election at the end of '72 was a significant one. There was more to it than the usual sordid bunfight. More at stake than 'Who will plunder whom?' Youthful lives were added to the chips. The yeas and nays were counted up, and suddenly The Draft was modern history. Former dodgers stepped into the light. It was a brand new day, no question... I hadn't seen much of Nick. He'd turned up for the second night of *Flying Start,* way back in July. Since then, I'd been to a couple of his gigs. We'd sort of lost touch. Just before Christmas, he sent me a telegram — Simon had phoned his place and left a contact number. It caught me on the hop. Nothing had been further from my thoughts. Not that I forget old friends, but time is time. I rushed out to the nearest booth...

"Yep?"

"... Simon?"

"Hang on."

Maybe half a minute slouched by. I wondered if he'd stopped using his fake surname yet.

"Doctor Mordecai speaking."

"Simon!"

"Is that Wanda? I can't believe it! Ten months I've had your note! I gave myself one chance in eight hundred! Where are you? What are you up to? I'm free, Wanda! We can do anything! You decide. Are you busy? What about right now? We'll have a feast. We'll go for a walk. You decide. Why aren't you saying anything? Are you angry? They can't touch me, Wanda! I'm legal! They can't do a thing! Are you coming over?"

"Where are you?"

"Home! You phoned *me,* don't forget. Do you remember how to get here?"

"You mean you're at The Rocks?"

"Yes! The Rocks. I've never left. I changed rooms once, to avoid Father's courier. Are you coming over? Do you like lobster? I know a — "

"I'll get a taxi. Wait out the front. I'd rather not deal with — "

"Bones? He's alright. He drinks a bit. So what? You should hear his stories. That guy's done just about — "

"Hang on, Simon. Give me half an hour."

"Okay, great! I'll go out the front!"

I caught a cab in King Street. I'd hardly strayed from Newtown during the recent weeks. Most days were spent working at home. Jake had my new script. He was still piecing together his dance parts. Rehearsals were set for mid-January. This show would be called *Leaps and Bounds.* I'd written a couple more songs. Lloyd had finally sent me a copy of the album. I'd played it at Jake's. It sounded pretty good to me, but sales hadn't been startling. Respectable, nothing more. At least my advance would be covered.

Sydney's traffic still amused me. There was something miraculous about it. The taxi squeezed into absurd spots, and wriggled out again even more easily. If you saw it in a movie, you'd scoff, you'd feel insulted. "Impossible!" you'd sneer. But here it was. In the flesh. Over and over, day and night. And no one even blinked. It was the status quo. If you didn't like it, you could vanish into the bush. Or you could go to sea...

I spotted Simon from a distance. His hands were stuck in his pockets and a cigarette hung on his lip. His beard had gone, but his hair was much longer. It covered his shoulders. And he'd obviously abandoned his grey dye sometime before. The cab drew up a few feet from him, but he didn't look across. I got the idea that his sight may have deteriorated further. I paid the driver and ran up to my old mate.

"Simon!"

"Aha!"

We inspected each other and laughed. I pulled his hair.

"It's real. Barbers tend to ask questions. They're really sneaky. They get you onto cricket, or a boat race, and before you know it, you've unloaded your darkest crimes in front of everyone. I've sworn off such a risk. Not *now* though. I'm an innocent party. I'll think about it. What have you been up to? I phoned Father earlier. I thought I'd better. Guess what. He's entering the lunatic arena. Carob-coated nuts and raisins. Hah! Do you know what carob is? A tree. You can forge a bogus chocolate from its pods. Guilt-free gluttony. Father predicts an illustrious future for it. He wants me to run the show. Hah! He's calling it the Natural Selection.

"Imagine it! Simon Mordecai, managing director. Not me! I've got a much better idea — *Doctor* Mordecai! I'm using the title already. I could go to prison! Only kidding. I don't mean a *medico*. Too much blood. *Mathematics,* Wanda! As soon as I get back to Melbourne I'm enrolling again. And I'll never leave university, I don't care how old I get. I'll bury myself in maths. You'll have to knock twice to reach me. Even the ceiling will have jottings on it. I've done that already in my room here. Calculations on every wall. Bones laughs. The owner's tolerant. He could paint fifty coats over it with the tips I've given him. *That* guy wasn't pleased about the election. Without me, he'll have to go back to three meals a day. Hah! At least he did the job, he kept his trap shut. He'll have to find another stooge now. It'll do him good.

"Heh! Father told me about Ruth! She'd better be out before I get back. Were you angry? Guess what! Shelley's in New York! A convention. Something to do with art and handlebars. Father couldn't stop laughing, he didn't make sense, he said he'd explain it later. But what's so funny? Shelley's work was always quite good…

"I must admit, I thought she'd have a better chance in music — There's always some kind of surprise, but not in mathematics, Wanda. No surprises, no deceptions…

"Heh! A favour. Don't make me talk about Bartos. You remember Bartos? I thought you would. Act like he didn't exist, okay? We don't invite him into our conversation. Do you like it here? You can come back to South Yarra if you want. Where do you live now?

"This harbour, that's what I like about Sydney. Nothing else. Maybe the Opera House. Have you seen it close up? A miracle. Soon people will be allowed in. There'll be concerts. Next year, I think. I might come back up for a look. The Jag's okay! Father stashed it in someone's shed. It's been on blocks, and warmed up now and then. I can't wait to drive it round Melbourne. Ruth had better be out of there!

"Who was the blond guy? I saw you that day. I heard you giving Bones money. I nearly came out, but I'd promised myself seclusion after... you know, the caper. 'Simon, you will hide from everyone, do you understand?' That's what I said to the mirror. 'No exceptions. Hide at least until you're legal.'

"I'm nuts. I realize that. I should have come out to see you. Wanda, my eyes are terrible. What if I can't drive? I'll have to ask somebody else. Maybe I'll ride in the back seat and smoke. I'll wear a homburg. 'There he goes!' they'll say. 'Doctor Mordecai of South Yarra.' But I can see my calculations okay, my numbers. They're in my head. Do you think I'll be able to drive, Wanda? What am I talking! I promised you a lobster, I remember now."

Simon took my arm and led me towards Circular Quay. He launched himself into other topics before I could speak. It didn't bother me. It was entertaining. It was Simon. I'd half expected to see a trembling shell.

We didn't stop at the waterfront. We headed up Pitt Street, and into the heart of the city. Not once did Simon break his monologue. Except to light up every ten minutes. Near Hyde Park, he pulled up suddenly and slapped his head. We'd walked too far. He led me back the way we'd come... Ah! Here it was. The place looked ordinary to me. But it had a reputation. The landlord had got to know all the right spots, from dining out frequently on Simon's bribes. The least the guy could do was to recommend a restaurant now and then. He'd apparently *raved* about this one. Simon hadn't followed it up till now.

We went in and ordered. The tirade continued till our meal arrived. The food lived up to its rap... I grabbed the chance to outline my own recent moves. And not so recent. Simon smoked and listened. He got excited. He was like a kid at a matinee. He had plenty of questions. I left out the sad bits. I guess there weren't that many. I'd been pretty lucky overall. Simon asked me again about returning to South Yarra. He knew I'd refuse. Because of Jake's theatre if nothing else. But I wouldn't have left Sydney anyway. I think I made that fairly clear... Dessert appeared. They'd got that right too. We'd been drinking champagne from the start. I nearly revealed the meaning of handlebars. I decided not to risk it. The joint wasn't fancy, but it was demure. Hysteria wouldn't have been at home.

We finally asked for the bill, and argued about whose shout it was. We flipped a coin. Simon won, and paid. We left quietly and headed for the harbour. A spin on the water seemed like an ace idea. Maybe over to the zoo or something... But we got lost in the rowdy streets. We were good and drunk. We hadn't realized.

Everything was hilarious — cars, pedestrians, cops. Buses in particular. We didn't need a handlebar story. I thought maybe Simon's father could tell it. He'd get a kick out of that.

About the Author

Wanda Koolmatrie was born in the far north of South Australia in 1949. Removed from her Pitjantjara mother in 1950, she was raised by foster parents in the western suburbs of Adelaide, where she went to school, leaving in 1966 and moving to the eastern states.

For the following three years she oscillated between being a factory worker and an autodidact, reading voluminously.

In 1973 she married Frank Koolmatrie, who died several years later. Since the mid 1970s she has travelled extensively in Australia. Her song lyrics have been performed in the U.S. She is currently living in London UK and among other things working on her next novel.